LANKY JONES

Also by Catherine Cookson

MRS. FLANNAGAN'S TRUMPET

GO TELL IT TO MRS. GOLIGHTLY

LANKY JONES

Catherine Cookson

Lothrop, Lee & Shepard Books
New York

Originally published in Great Britain in 1980 by Macdonald Futura Publishers.

First U.S. Edition
1 2 3 4 5 6 7 8 9 10

Library of Congress Cataloging in Publication Data

Cookson, Catherine.
Lanky Jones.

SUMMARY: A 15-year-old and his divorced father become stranded and are offered refuge by a kind family in their farm house where they hear screams in the night, meet a threatening character, and eventually encounter vicious sheep thieves.
[1. England—Fiction. 2. Divorce—Fiction.
3. Mystery and detective stories] I. Title.
PZ7.C775Lan [Fic] 80-22676
ISBN 0-688-00430-X ISBN 0-688-00431-8 (lib. bdg.)

1

"Dad."

"Yes."

"May I ask you a question?"

"You don't often ask if you can ask a question. What is it?"

"Do you still love Mom?"

The car swerved slightly; the driver turned the wheel sharply before answering briefly, "No."

"Did . . . did you love her at the time she left you?"

There was a longer pause now before Peter Jones answered, "No."

"Is . . . is that why she went off and left you . . . us?"

Mr. Jones pressed his back tight against the leather seat and let out a long breath before he said, "And the answer for the third time is no. But now I'm going to ask you a question. Why were you in such a devil of a rush to come back home? You haven't been like that during your other visits to her."

There was no pause before Daniel jerked his head toward his father and exclaimed in bitter tones, "*He* wasn't there at other times."

"But you had met him before, and, as far as I can gather, you didn't think he was such a bad type."

"He wasn't married to her then and acting as if he owned her, and the house and me too."

"Oh"—the word was long drawn out—"played the father figure to the fifteen-year-old stepson, did he?"

"Yes, and overdid it."

There was silence in the car now except for the noise from the engine, which was indeed a noise. Being a 1954 Morris, it had seen its better days, and every now and again the rhythm of the engine was broken by a sound like a protest from an old body being driven beyond its limits. But both the father and the son seemed oblivious to all but their own thoughts, which were dwelling on the same person.

Daniel's memory was taking him back to 1958 when he was eight years old—that was when he first became aware that his mother was very smart, very vivacious. It was at the school play and Jimmy Osborn had said to him, "Boy! Your mom's a knockout."

He did not know at what age he had become aware that his mom was a person who easily became bored. Perhaps it was that time when she had danced him around the room, saying in a sing-song voice, "Your dad doesn't realize your mom's a song and dance girl." He could see his father sitting in the armchair smoking his pipe. He had just said he wasn't going out to the club or anywhere else that night.

Looking back, Daniel thought perhaps that was the first time his mother had gone out on her own. He had considered his dad to be silly and selfish not to take her out; but then his dad, being a gardener, was outside all day and so what he looked forward to, at least for one or two nights a week, was a quiet evening at home.

When was it he had realized he was on his dad's side? Soon after his mother had started to go out every night, he supposed; that was after she had gone back full time to office work. Previous to that she had always been home when he had come back from school and she would be preparing a meal. But after she'd started work again he had had to let himself into the house and set the table for supper, which usually meant beans or fish-sticks.

Then just over two years ago she had walked out. He hadn't heard any big fight or anything like that; she had merely left a letter to say that she wasn't coming back.

Although his dad had just said he hadn't loved her when she left him, he now recalled that his dad had hardly spoken for a week afterward except in monosyllables. But when he did get around to talking, the first thing he had said to him was, "You didn't want to go with her, did you?" and when he'd answered, "No," his father had said, "That's all right then."

Although he liked being with his dad, there were times when he felt very lonely, as if he were missing something. His mind wouldn't allow him to put the word "loving" to his need because his mom had never been loving toward him; she had never put her arms around him and hugged him. He knew it was soppy to expect a mother to do that, yet some mothers did, he had seen them, even with fellows as tall and as lanky as he was. He wished he wasn't so lanky; he wished he could stop growing. He was sprouting so quickly that at times he didn't know where to put his arms or legs.

His mom's new man joked about his height, all the time pretending he was angry that he was taller than him. There was an arrangement whereby he had to visit his mother once a month. Well, when the time came around for his next excursion to Carlisle he'd be sick in some way, perhaps break one of his gangly limbs.

"I wonder if that cottage has been sold. You remember the cottage?"

He looked at his father. Yes, he remembered the cottage, or what was left of it; it was a wreck standing in the middle of a field. One day in the summer when they were up here his father had walked around it as if he were viewing a palace. All his father seemed to want was a cottage in the country and a piece of land. But he himself hoped his dad never realized his dream, not out here anyway in this wild, sparsely populated part of the country, where all you saw were little stone farmhouses dotted here and there.

"I said, do you remember the cottage?"

"Yes, I remember the . . . the ruin."

Mr. Jones laughed now, saying, "Ruin or not, I bet somebody's had the same idea I had and snipped it." He leaned forward and peered out of the windshield onto the narrow, snow-bordered road as he said, "We're nearing the turnoff. What do you say we go and have a look at it?"

It was Daniel's turn to laugh now as he asked, "Are you looking for trouble, Dad? The side roads will likely be blocked, and Jinny's been grunting more than usual. Perhaps you haven't heard her."

Daniel shook his head as he watched his father take his hand from the wheel and pat the dashboard, saying with real affection, "She's been grunting for years, and if I know anything she'll go on grunting when some of this year's products are on the scrap heap. Well, what do you say?"

Mr. Jones glanced at his son and Daniel answered brightly, "Yes, I don't mind. If we go into a snowdrift there's half a flask of tea and two sandwiches left; they should see us over the next week or until they come and dig us out."

They laughed together now and both sat up straighter in their seats, peering along the road looking for the turning. When they came to it, Mr. Jones swung the wheel, saying, "Here goes!" and Daniel, his tone high and light, shouted, "You know what you sounded like there, Dad? Like a canoeist approaching the rapids, knowing he would be lucky if he ever got through."

"Well, these are no rapids; look ahead, there's been farm tractors up here. It's clearer than the main road in parts."

After about half a mile there was a sharp bend in the road, and this at the top of a steep gradient, and the expression on both their faces changed somewhat when they saw the road at the bottom was covered with thick snow.

Before they actually reached the level ground Mr. Jones drew the car to a stop and, looking to the right of him, pointed, saying, "There it is!"

"Yes"—Daniel nodded—"and by all appearance nobody's jumped at the chance of taking it. What on earth can you see in it, Dad?"

"Oh, a home, a smallholding, a way of life."

"You're not going to get out and have another walk around it, are you, not in weather like this?"

"No." Mr. Jones smiled as he shook his head. Then he started the car again, saying, "I'll run down to that field gate; there's more room for turning."

A minute later, having backed successfully and apparently with no trouble toward the gate, he went to drive forward again, but the back wheels whizzed and the car shuddered. "Oh no!" Daniel cried as he swung around and looked out of the rear window; then he added dolefully, "The back wheels are in a drift, Dad."

"Good Lord! Look. Get out, get behind her, and when I tell you, push . . . lift and push."

"Just like that?"

His father nodded at him, saying, "Yes, just like that."

For the next ten minutes Mr. Jones yelled, "Push! Push! Push!" And Daniel attempted to lift and push until he became exhausted. Leaning over the trunk. he finally called, "It's no good, Dad, she's going in deeper. We'll have to get some help."

Mr. Jones now came out of the car, stood on the roadway, and gazed about him. Then, looking at his wristwatch, he said, "And we'll have to have it soon. It's well past three; it will be dark in no time. Good Lord!" He shook his head. "I must have been crazy to come down here."

"You said it." Daniel nodded at him. "It looks as if you'll have your cottage after all; we might have to camp out there."

"Don't be silly. There'll be a farm round here somewhere. Let's go and see."

They walked over the packed snow, went around three more bends in the lane, and then they saw the farm. It was about half a mile distant and situated at the bottom of the valley, closer to the opposite hills, which seemed to go on until they disappeared into the sky.

"They'll have a tractor."

"Yes, likely." Daniel nodded at his father, then added, "But they mightn't like the idea of lending it; they'll think we're a pair of idiots to get stuck in a drift."

"And they're right, aren't they?" Mr. Jones made a slow conciliatory shrug of his shoulders, which caused Daniel to laugh as he answered, "Speak for yourself. I didn't want to look at that wreck of a cottage."

Their first impression of the farm was that everything looked very tidy; their second, that everything was very quiet except for the bleating of some sheep that were penned in a field near the outbuildings.

They crossed a paved yard and came to what was evidently the back door of the house. Mr. Jones knocked, then stood waiting.

There was no response and so he knocked louder. When again no one came to answer, he tentatively lifted the old-fashioned latch and pressed against the door.

"It's locked. They're out."

"Well, I shouldn't imagine they'll be out for long, if they've got cattle to see to."

Mr. Jones stood looking about him, then said, "Sheep look after themselves mostly."

"There's cows over there. I heard one mooing," said Daniel.

His father listened, then said, "Yes, you're right. It must be near milking time. Anyway, I can't see the point of standing here. Let's get back to the car; we can wait in it until they come along."

"What if there's another road?"

"I don't think so. There's only a narrow path leading up to the hills; they wouldn't use that. Come along."

They were both cold and shivering when they returned to the car, and after finishing the tea from the flask and the last of the sandwiches, they prepared themselves to wait. But they had hardly settled down when they heard the rumbling of a vehicle approaching, and they were out and standing by the hood of their own car when the Land-Rover came around the bend and drew up in front of them.

They looked up at the young man who was driving, and at the two faces beyond his, those of a woman and a young girl. It was the woman who spoke. "Stuck?" she said.

"Yes, Ma, they've gotten stuck." It was the young man, laughing now, who answered her. Then he turned to them and said, "What you doing down here, anyway? You come to see us?"

"No." Mr. Jones shook his head. "I . . . well, really"—he gave a shamefaced grin—"I came to have a second look at that old cottage." He jerked his head backward.

"That!" The young man screwed up his face. "What on earth for?"

"I couldn't really tell you, except I . . . I saw it in the summer and just wondered if anyone round about had yet taken it."

"No." The young man shook his head. "Well, you see, they wouldn't because they are all sane around here."

Daniel wanted to laugh—they had come across a joker.

When the Land-Rover door was pushed open and the young man jumped to the ground, Daniel saw that the stranger was almost a head shorter than he and looked not so much a young man as a boy, perhaps about his own age. Yet he reasoned he must be seventeen to be driving a car.

"Have you got any rope?"

He was looking at Daniel, and Daniel answered, "No."

The young man now went around to the back of the Land-Rover, saying, "Don't you ever listen to the television or the radio? They tell you never to go out in this weather without a rope, a shovel, a pick, and enough grub to last you a month."

"Don't take any notice of him." The woman had now gotten down onto the road. She was of medium height and was wearing a green velour coat with a fur-lined hood attached, and the face looking out from it was pretty and kindly. She was oldish, as old as his mother, he thought, well over thirty, but her voice was light and had the laughing quality of her son. She was looking at his father, saying now, "Have you been stranded long?"

"About an hour or so," Mr. Jones replied. "We . . . we called at your farm. You are from the farm?" He pointed.

"Yes. It isn't often we go out but my husband is in the hospital in Hexham and . . . and we all wanted to see him."

"Oh, I'm sorry. I hope it's nothing serious?"

She paused before answering, "He . . . he's much better now. We hope to have him home soon."

"That's good."

"Well, would you like to get in before dark or would you rather stay put?"

Mr. Jones was forced to laugh and he turned to see Daniel tying a rope under the front bumper and the young man mounting his cab again.

After a series of stops and starts and some pushing from behind, in which the woman and her daughter helped, the back wheels eventually left the drift and were once again on firm ground.

"Thank you, thank you very much indeed." Mr. Jones was looking at the young man. "I'm indeed grateful."

"That's all right. Pity we didn't come along sooner. Have you far to go?"

"Newcastle."

"Oh, you won't make that before dark, will you?"

"No."

"Have you plenty of gas?"

"Yes, I always keep a full tank."

"Well then, turn her round and I'll see you up the bank. What I mean is, I'll see if she can get up the bank. It's freezing, you know. It's a sheet of ice up at the top now."

Mr. Jones nodded from one to the other and again said, "Thanks," after which Daniel, looking at the young man, said, "It's good of you," and he included the woman in his thanks. Then his eyes rested on the girl, who was staring at him. She was like her mother, with brown hair and blue eyes.

He was feeling embarrassed under her stare and he said again, "Thanks. Ta," before turning around and getting into the car.

When Mr. Jones turned the key in the ignition, the result was a choked spurt, a grunt, then silence.

Putting his foot down hard on the accelerator, he tried again. After the third time he glanced apprehensively at Daniel and, the color rising in his face, he muttered, "Oh no. No!"

After the fifth attempt he wound down the window and looked at the face of the young man, whose countenance too looked solemn except that there was a deep twinkle in the back of the eyes.

"Often have this trouble?"

"No, never before."

"She's an old 'un." The young man now looked toward the hood as if he were discussing a horse or some farm creature, then added, "Ten years old?"

"No, eleven."

"Old age tantrums, I should say. Well, try her again."

A little peeved, Mr. Jones foolishly rammed his foot down on the accelerator once more; then again and again and again.

"Know anything about cars, I mean their insides?"

"Very little," said Mr. Jones.

"Mind if I have a look?"

"Not at all." . . .

They were all standing in the road again; the hood was up and the young man was poking about among the wires. Presently he said, "Nothing that I can see wrong there; it must be something deep in her bowels."

Deep in her bowels. If the situation hadn't been serious, Daniel would have burst out laughing.

"It's getting dark." It was the first time the girl had spoken. Her voice was different from her mother's and brother's, markedly so. Her words were softly spoken.

"Yes, it is." Her mother nodded now and, turning to Mr. Jones, she said, "Would you like to come up to the house? It's no good standing out here freezing."

"Oh, we don't want to put you to any trouble. Is . . . is there a garage anywhere near?"

"Yes." It was the young man speaking again. "Two miles away. No, three. Yes, three"—he nodded to himself—"in Bardon Mill. Aw, leave it. Nobody can do anything with her tonight. And look, as Sally said it's getting dark and I can tell you for nothing, no garage hand's coming out at this time of night, especially on a Saturday, and it promising to snow again at any minute. So come on. Bring whatever you need out of there"—he thumbed toward the car—"and let's get moving."

As if each were obeying an elder, they both took out their bags from the trunk and obediently got into the back of the Land-Rover; and seemingly within a split second they had bounded over the rough road and landed in the farmyard. They were inside the house within minutes and Daniel saw the kitchen of Hillburn Farm for the first time. And there came over him the most odd feeling, a terrifyingly odd feeling.

Perhaps it was the sudden heat of the room after the cold outside that had brought it on again. Twice before he'd experienced this same feeling. Once, when his mother thrashed him for no reason he could see except that he was playing his records. He had played one three times because he liked it; it was an oldie by Jim Reeves called "I Can't Stop Loving You." They were bringing a lot of oldies back at the club, besides Elvis. She had seemed to go berserk. The second time he had felt like this was the night she left them. On both occasions he had cried; and now he wanted to cry again. . . . But why?

2

It was two hours later, yet it seemed to Daniel that he had been in this farm kitchen-cum-living room for two days, two weeks, two years, for the place and people seemed so familiar to him now that he might have been acquainted with them all his life.

The room was stone-flagged and had an open fireplace, yet also modern amenities, from a fridge and washing machine to a brand-new stove, from the oven of which Mrs. Everton, as he now knew her to be, had sometime earlier taken a large casserole dish bubbling with brown dumplings. The meal was so good that Daniel couldn't remember having tasted anything like it before.

He had learned that the young man's name was Michael, and the hilarity that he had caused at the meal bore out Daniel's first impression of his being a joker. But Daniel also learned that he was a hard-working joker. As soon as they had entered the house he had disappeared, only to reappear minutes later in working clothes and accompanied by his sister, who had also changed her clothes.

It was their mother who explained they were bound for the cow barns, saying as she busied herself around the kitchen, "It's routine. You've got to stick to it on a farm. Animals have their own time and they see that you learn it."

For over half an hour he had sat in a deep leather chair to the side of the open fire at the end of the room and listened to his father and Mrs. Everton in conversation. He learned that Mr. Everton had been in the hospital for three weeks with kidney trouble, and apparently it wasn't his first visit there. There had been a sadness in Mrs. Everton's voice as she said, "He should have had himself seen to ages ago, but he wouldn't give in until Michael left school and was able to take over."

"You are lucky to have him then," his father had replied, and to this Mrs. Everton said, "And I know it and I thank God for him." And then she added, "You might get the impression that he's light-minded because of his joking manner, but he has a serious side, and I've known times when I've longed to hear him joke. That was during his last year at school when he realized how much his father needed him here full time. He and his father are great pals, and it's odd you know—" Daniel had watched her stop laying the cutlery on the table and look toward his father as she added, "My husband hasn't the slightest sense of humor. We could be roaring our heads off at something we had seen on the television but there he would be sitting straight-faced. Michael used to say he'd given up laughing for Lent."

Daniel couldn't believe that they were to stay here

tonight, but it seemed to have been a foregone conclusion since they had entered the house, for after they'd had the meal Michael had said, "I'll take you upstairs and show you where you are to sleep."

His father had protested politely, saying, "But it's an imposition. I . . . I never expected—" only to be cut short by Michael saying bluntly, "Where did you expect to sleep then, out in your four-wheeled monument? Or in Ramsey's ruin?" Apparently Ramsey's ruin was the cottage, which had once belonged to a man of that name.

The bedroom was one of four leading off a square landing. The landing itself, Daniel noticed, was bigger than their own sitting room, and when, standing in the middle of it, he voiced this as he looked around him, Michael said, "The house is much bigger than it looks from the outside." Pointing to where another staircase led upward, he said, "There are three big attic rooms up there too. That's where we keep the family ghost, and the heirlooms. And mind, we search everybody before they leave."

As Michael switched on the light and led the way into the bedroom Daniel thought that he might just get a bit tired of this young fellow's wisecracking; like the saying, you can get too much of a good thing. He wondered if Michael ever talked in an ordinary way, without joking and all.

The bedroom was solidly and well furnished, which Michael pointed out, saying, "Best room in the house, this. The only thing is it faces north and is inclined to be a bit nippy in the winter. Anyway, there're plenty of blankets." He thumbed toward the bed. Then going toward the door and pointing, he said, "Usual offices right opposite."

"Thank you. Thank you very much," Mr. Jones said.

The door had hardly closed before it was opened again and their young host, putting his head around it, said, "Don't go to bed yet; 'tisn't every night we have four for cards and I can do some fleecing. . . . Do some fleecing!" He pulled a face before closing the door again.

Finally left alone, Mr. Jones looked at Daniel and, pulling a wry face now himself, said, "What is known as a smart lad," at the same time drawing the side of his forefinger across the bottom of his nose; and as Daniel laughed, he protested in a whisper, "Oh, don't you start, Dad. Two of you would be one too many, in fact two too many."

"Watch out, you're at it as well."

Daniel smiled, then said, "But they are kind, very kind. His mother's nice, isn't she?"

"Yes, yes, she's a very nice woman, I should say, and so is the girl. Why didn't you talk to her?"

"Oh, I don't know. I . . . I suppose it's because she didn't have much to say herself, and she has that soft way of talking."

"Yes, I noticed that, at first at least. But after a while her voice changed and she was speaking ordinarily. I think perhaps she's shy. Well now, let's get sorted out." And as Mr. Jones opened his bag he added, "I think I'll take my jacket off and put a sweater on. What about you?"

"What? Yes, oh yes, me too." But before Daniel opened his bag he stopped and looked at his father and said, "It's been a strange day, hasn't it? At least it has for me. There was an awful fight with Mom when she knew I'd phoned for you. And that fellow of hers talking father talk at me; he made me sick. And then the car breaking down, and meeting these kind people and landing in this farmhouse. It's so peaceful here, isn't it? I never wanted to live in the country, as you know, but this is different." And as his father smiled at him he added, "Shall I use the bathroom first?"

"Yes, go on."

Daniel now went onto the landing and was crossing to the door opposite when he was brought around sharply by a conversation taking place on the stairs. There was a light in the hall down below and it showed up the head and shoulders of both the brother and sister of the house. Michael had his back toward him and was standing on the step above Sally. She was saying in a pleading tone, "You won't, Michael? Oh, you won't?" And Michael's hissing reply came to Daniel, saying, "No, I won't. All right, I told you, I won't." And on this he put his hands on his sister's shoulders and shook her; then, turning her about, he pushed her down the two stairs into the hall below. Whether Michael was about to follow her or make his way up the stairs Daniel didn't wait to see, but he almost sprang to the bathroom door and, pushing it open, entered, then stood with his hands behind him on the knob, his teeth nipping his lower lip as he asked himself what it was all about. Sally had seemed frightened. Why was she pleading with her brother like that? And his treatment of her had been anything but gentle. Just a minute ago he had been thinking all was peace and tranquility in this house, but that incident had given no evidence of peace and tranquility, much the reverse.

It had been a strange day, a very strange day.

They were in bed early, just before ten. As Mrs. Everton had said, they went to bed early because the day started early on a farm. His father and Mrs. Everton had talked quite a lot during the evening. She hadn't played cards but had sat by the fireside, knitting, and when she made any remark his father would turn from the table and answer her very pleasantly. This had prompted Michael eventually to ask, "Are you going to play cards or are you going to talk?" And they had all laughed.

Daniel told himself he couldn't make this young fellow out, because he had spoken civilly to his sister during the evening, in a way that made it appear as though he could never be rough with her.

Daniel liked Sally; he thought her a nice little girl. He thought of her as little but she was thirteen. And yet she didn't act like the thirteen-year-olds he knew at school. Oh boy, no. Take Susan Dooley, for instance. Half the boys were crazy about her and she knew it. But with Sally there was a sort of . . . He hunted around in his mind for a word to define her. Then he felt slightly embarrassed as the word "innocent" came to him. She had talked quite normally all evening; in fact, once or twice she had made them all laugh. It had been quite a nice evening on the whole.

He turned in the bed, about to make a remark on the evening to his father, when a gentle snort told him that his father was already asleep. Daniel shook his head slowly. He didn't know how his father did it, but as soon as he put his head down he was off. He remembered his mother's complaining about it in a way that was joking yet wasn't funny. His father had once explained that, being out in the air most days, he found no difficulty in sleeping at night.

Daniel himself could never get to sleep right away; his mind always seemed to go around in circles about the day's doings. Especially so after a day at school if anything had happened, such as a fight. That time two years ago when they had formed gangs and he wouldn't join either of them, he had hardly slept properly for a week. It was after his mother had left home and he was feeling in a state. But even if she had still been at home he wouldn't have joined a gang. He'd had to thank his height for the fact that he wasn't beaten up by either of them.

It was odd when he came to think about that. Because he was big they all thought he must be tough. If only they knew what went on inside his head and that most of the time he was scared to death, they would have floored him before now.

When he was small he had only to witness any kind of fight in the street and he would make a dash for home. It was fortunate, he thought, that he now had his height to cover his real feelings. Little fellows seemed to have more spunk than the big ones. There was Tommy Thirkell. Tom Thumb, they used to call him. One and another of them had pushed him about for a long time. Tommy used to come and stand near him as if his height would give him protection. Then one day half a dozen of them had collared him in the corner of the schoolyard and all of a sudden he seemed to go mad, for he broke loose from them and grabbed a skipping rope from a girl and turned and faced them. And boy, did he make them jump! The end of the rope caught one of the fellows around the neck and nearly throttled him. The outcome was, Tommy's father was called to the school, and it was rumored he did practically the same to the headmaster, except he used words. But from then on Tommy was left alone. He was another one that wouldn't join a gang.

Daniel's thoughts drifted away around the question he often asked himself at night: why, being so tall and well made, should he be so afraid of fights? Was he a coward? What would happen to him if there was a war and he had to go and fight? Now Michael, the fellow he had met today, he would have no trouble with such thoughts; he would go in with his fists flailing. He could just see him.

He was seeing him as he drifted into sleep.

He had no notion of what part of the night it was. He had slept soundly; he was still sleeping soundly when the scream went right through his head and brought his eyes and mouth open again, and he hadn't time to ask himself if he had been dreaming when there it was again, a weird, awful scream. And he was sitting bolt upright in bed when it happened for the third time, but more distant now, only this time it was followed by a noise that sounded like a prolonged groan.

"Dad! Dad!" He was shaking his father roughly by the shoulders. "Dad! Wake up."

"What? What's the matter? What is it?" His father had turned onto his back.

"Didn't you hear it, the screaming?"

Mr. Jones came awake all of a sudden. Turning onto his side now and pushing at Daniel, he hissed somewhat roughly, "Don't be an idiot. Screaming . . . what are you talking about? You've been dreaming, boy."

"I wasn't dreaming, Dad. Somebody was screaming."

Mr. Jones himself sat bolt upright now and listened. There was no sound whatever; they were enveloped in blackness and silence. They sat like this for some minutes until Daniel said, "Shall I put on the light?"

"No; best you can do is get yourself to sleep. The screams are likely the result of the food you've had tonight; you're not used to such home-cooked meals. Go on, get yourself down and go to sleep. That's what I'm going to do, and if you hear any more screams, take them in your stride and don't wake me." On this Mr. Jones flopped down onto his side, pulled the blankets well up over his shoulders and under his chin, and in hardly any time at all he was again gently snorting.

Daniel lay tense, his ears strained for any kind of noise, but the only sound that came to him was that of a dog fox barking in the distance. That was, until he heard a kind of creak coming from the direction of the ceiling. It was as if someone had trodden on an uneven floorboard.

There it was again. Someone was moving about in the attics. Yet nobody was supposed to be up there. Mrs. Everton's bedroom was next door, Sally's was next to the bathroom—he had seen her go in sometime earlier—and Michael's was the end room. His door was the closest to the stairs.

Now that was a funny thing. Surely, if he himself had heard the screams, Mrs. Everton would have, or Sally, or again Michael, but there had been no movement whatever until that creaking sound above a few seconds ago.

There was something fishy here. There it was again, further away, but nevertheless someone walking on the floor above.

Within seconds he was out of bed and groping toward the door. Having found the handle, he gripped it and turned it very, very slowly, then gently opened the door about an inch or two. He didn't know what to expect at this stage. The landing was as black as the room he was standing in, at least it seemed to be. But then he saw a faint ray of dimmed light coming from the end of the landing where the stairs led up to the attics. He now pushed the door further closed until it afforded him only an eye's width, but it was enough for him to see the present head of the house, as Michael seemed to infer he was, come tiptoeing past the doors, a flashlight in one hand and something else in the other. Daniel narrowed his gaze in an effort to make out what the thing was. It looked like a ruler, yet not quite as long; but it wasn't made of wood, at least not varnished wood. In the light of the flashlight the thing looked white, bone white, and held in the fist as it was it took on the appearance of a weapon.

Daniel didn't move until Michael's door had closed on him; then he waited a full minute before he dared to turn the handle and shut his own door. Groping his way back to the bed, he got into it and lay shivering while curbing the desire to awaken his father once again, for what could he say to him? Except that he had seen the young man of the house coming down from the attic carrying a light in one hand and some object in the other.

But why had Michael been up in the attic at this time of night? Why? And the screams he had heard he knew had come from that direction. Was there someone in the house besides the three people he had already met, and was it someone who had to be knocked into silence?

Before his eyes there arose the white stick or whatever implement, a weapon.

Oh, if only the morning were here and they could make their way home. There was something fishy going on and, although part of him hated to admit it, he wanted no further knowledge of it. There was the same feeling in him now as there was when he saw the gangs fighting: he wanted to get as far away as possible from the danger. And he sensed danger here, a weird kind of danger that was impossible to figure out.

It had certainly been a strange day yesterday; it was

now a strange night, and it was going to be a long one because he would never be able to sleep after this.

He sprang upward in the bed as a hand grasped his shoulder. "Come on, come on, wake up and get your tea." Daniel gasped as he looked up into his father's face, then turned his head toward a white light that was blinding him. Mrs. Everton was pulling open the curtains and saying as she did so, "I'm glad you slept well. But I've got news for you—it's snowing." She turned toward the bed, addressing herself now to Mr. Jones as she went on, "I'm afraid there'll be very little hope of anybody coming out to fix your car today. But you said last night you have to get back for work tomorrow, so Michael suggested he give you a run into Hexham when he goes after breakfast to see his father. They let us in at odd times," she explained, "when the weather is bad like this. They know how difficult the roads are out here. And so he's going in on his own. The Land-Rover can get through most things, yet I've known the snowdrifts so high that it's been stuck too. And about your car. Michael will see that it's taken to a garage and as soon as it's ready I'll give you a ring. Are you in the phone book? I forgot to ask."

"Yes." Mr. Jones nodded at her, then added, "It's very kind of you and I feel we've put you to a lot of trouble."

"Not at all, not at all. Drink your tea before it gets cold. Breakfast will be in half an hour."

When the door closed on her Daniel stared toward it, for the thought had come to him that she hadn't smiled once—in fact, her face was strained; she looked tired. Last night she had looked pleasant and she had laughed all the time at her son's jokes. When she had sat with her arm around her daughter and with Sally's head snuggled into her, she had been the picture of what he imagined a mother should be. But this morning she looked different.

"Look, drink your tea. What's the matter with you?" His father had twisted around on the bed and was looking into his face, and he said in an undertone, "You're not still thinking about hearing screams, are you?"

Looking back into his father's eyes, Daniel was a second before replying, and then he said emphatically, "Just that —and more."

"What more?" Mr. Jones's voice was very low, and Daniel muttered as he swung his legs out of bed, "I'll . . . I'll tell you later, when we get out of here."

"Don't talk like that, when we get out of here. To my mind we've never been treated so kindly in our lives. She's a woman I'd call real neighborly. And the young fellow too. Oh"—he shook his head from side to side— "he's a wisecracker, I grant you, but he's young and he'll grow out of that."

"I hope he grows out of other things as well."

Mr. Jones, himself now out of bed, stood looking across the room to where Daniel was pulling on his clothes, and he nipped at his lower lip as if to prevent himself speaking. He had never seen the boy like this before; he was always so grateful for the smallest kindness shown to him. It was true his mother hadn't in the past killed him with kindness; in fact, she seemed more concerned about him now since she had taken on her new life. Perhaps for the first time she was realizing she had a son and was now missing him. But the boy, he wasn't given to fancies and he seemed positive he had heard screams. And what was this something more he hinted at? Well, it was no good probing now. Daniel could be stubborn when he liked. He'd have to wait till they got away. . . .

It was a fine breakfast—bacon, eggs, sausages, and fried bread. Daniel had thought he didn't feel like eating, but he cleared his plate because it wasn't often he had a breakfast like this. The others had apparently eaten because the table was set for two only.

They hadn't as yet seen either Michael or Sally, and Mrs. Everton seemed busy elsewhere, so they didn't see much of her either until they were ready to go. It was then that Mr. Jones asked, "How much do I owe you, Mrs. Everton?"

"Oh, nothing at all."

"Oh, but . . . but we must pay something. I mean, we've had much more than bed and breakfast." He laughed now.

"It was an emergency: you didn't expect to come and . . . and we've been glad to have you. It's been good company." She nodded from one to the other and now she did smile.

"It's very kind of you, but I still feel . . ."

"Say no more about it. But if you are ever this way again we'll be pleased to see you. And I'll phone you when I have news of the car. Though if it keeps snowing like this it could be some time before they can get it up the hill even with a tow. It could be that from tonight we'll be snowed in ourselves."

"You must have a very hard time of it with the cattle when that happens."

"Yes, 'tis the cattle that suffer most. But we've been fortunate, and Michael is far-seeing and he's brought most of ours down to the low field."

"Well, for their sakes and yours I hope we have a thaw

pretty soon. Good-bye, Mrs. Everton, and thank you very much indeed."

"Good-bye, Mr. Jones. Oh, and by the way, I didn't like to inquire but . . . but when you said that your son here"—she inclined her head toward Daniel—"had been visiting his mother in Carlisle, I . . . I wondered, is your home actually there and you work in Newcastle or . . . ?" She paused, looking rather bemused, and Mr. Jones replied quietly, "Daniel visits his mother now and again in Carlisle. We're divorced; have been for two years."

"Oh. Oh, I'm very sorry. I didn't mean to pry, I just wondered about Daniel still going to school in Newcastle. Well"—she spread out her hands—"curiosity killed the cat. I'm not really nosy."

"No, of course not. And I quite understand your wondering. Well, we must be off. I can see your son's got the Land-Rover out in the yard and if I'm any judge of character, if we're not there on the dot he'll go off without us." He laughed now, and she smiled at him, saying, "He . . . he appears very brash at times, but he's not really."

"Oh, I didn't mean to criticize. I think he's a fine young fellow, someone you can be very proud of."

"I am."

They were outside in the yard now and Michael greeted them both with a single word, "Morning." The word sounded curt and was said in a manner one might have expected from a taciturn and reserved young man, not from the voluble joker of last night.

"Good-bye, Mrs. Everton. And thank you very much."

"Good-bye, Daniel. It's been very nice having you."

Daniel was about to say, "Please say good-bye to Sally for me," when a movement at a window directly above the kitchen window caught his eye and, looking up, he saw the white, sad-looking face of a young girl. Even as he recognized it was Sally's, he also recognized that she too had changed, more so even than her mother or her brother. And his mouth fell slightly agape when he saw the lower part of her face looked contorted; then during the second before she moved from the window he made out that her lower lip was split.

"Daniel." His father's voice brought him around. Mr. Jones had his foot on the step of the Land-Rover about to swing himself upward and he asked, "Are you going in the middle?"

"No." Daniel shook his head firmly. "I prefer the door seat, if you don't mind."

"Not me; it'll be warmer in the middle." His father laughed.

At the moment Daniel wasn't wanting any physical contact with Michael Everton; in fact he didn't want contact of any kind with him, for he was piecing together the events of the night: the incident on the stairs; Sally's begging her brother not to do something; the screams; then that white implement. And yet it hadn't been very big, not as long as a ruler. Would that have caused a busted lip? No, more like somebody's fist. Yet even had Sally been hit she wouldn't have screamed like that, not again and again and again.

Oh, he would be glad when he got away from this place. Last night, compared with his home in Newcastle it had seemed to be heaven, but now everything was reversed—his home seemed a safe, sane place. The only screams you heard in their district were from somebody's television.

Michael slowed the Land-Rover as they neared the car

and he had to drive almost into the ditch in order to pass it.

"Poor old girl, she's nearly buried now." Mr. Jones leaned forward and peered through the falling snow at his car, which had been like a companion to him for years.

"It would pay you to let it go for scrap." As he spoke Michael applied gentle pressure on the accelerator. The Land-Rover ground its way up the steep bank, and it wasn't until they reached the top that Mr. Jones answered him, saying, "I'm rather fond of the old girl."

Michael said nothing further and for quite some time no one spoke. But as they neared the main road Michael leaned forward and peered through the windshield wipers to where a man was plodding toward them, and what he muttered now was not understandable to Mr. Jones or to Daniel.

"Things always happen in three's and here's the second of them," he said.

When the truck came to a stop close to where the man was standing, his Wellington boots almost up to their tops in a drift, Michael rolled down the window and without any preamble said, "Dad's not here. He's in the hospital."

"Aye, that's what I heard, so I thought I'd come down and see Mary. Perhaps she'd like a hand."

"I'm managing all right; no need to trouble."

"No trouble at all, Michael boy. Nothing's ever been a trouble to do things for your dad or he for me. What's mates for? Where you off to?"

"The hospital."

"Oh; then it's no use waiting for you to turn around and take me down. Still, I've made it afore in worse weathers than this. Be seein' you. Tell John I'll be in to see him, and not to worry, I'll help out."

The window was wound up with a slam. Tl
Rover almost seemed to leave the ground, and t
some way along the main road when Michael,
at Mr. Jones and with no aggressiveness in his vc
said, "Funny, you always get offers of help that
do without."

"You're not very fond of him?" Mr. Jones's
was quiet and Michael grunted "Huh!" before an
"Fond? I hate his guts. I've always been able tc
stink a mile off, yet it's funny, my dad's a very sens
except where he's concerned, for he could never
thing wrong in him. Apparently they met when tl
doing their National Service and became what
calls bosom pals. He'll neither work nor want, t
Never kept a job down in years. Lives on social
and periodically turns up here. I can never unc
Dad's putting up with him."

"Wartime relationships are very strange."

"There was no war on; it was all over, so I gatl
to hear him talk, he won it all on his own." He
for a moment, and then, his voice dropping, he s
only wants the third thing to happen, and I kno
coming."

It was on the tip of Daniel's tongue to say,
thing connected with the screams in the night?" w
was shocked to hear Michael add, "For my father i
to die."

There was silence in the cab now except for the
bing of the engine; then Mr. Jones said quietly, "
You mean there's no hope?"

"That's what I mean. He's got a liver complaint
thinks he's getting better and will be home soon
never be home again. I . . . I saw the doctor last

he told me what to expect."

Again there was silence. And now Daniel bent slightly forward to look past his father and at the sharp profile of the seventeen-year-old boy who was a man already, and he found that once again his opinion of this new acquaintance was changing. He could like the young man who was driving this truck, yet he didn't like the young fellow who shook his sister roughly, nor the one who had crept down from the attic stairs with that small white implement in his hand. Then there was the fellow who wisecracked until he began to get on your nerves. Michael Everton was a mixture right enough, and it came to Daniel that he wouldn't like to cross him in any way. Well, he wouldn't be called upon to do that, would he? because he had no intention of visiting his farm ever again.

It was amazing the number of different characters he had come across this weekend, from his mother's new husband to the three people at the farm, not forgetting the man they had just passed. Oh, he'd be glad when he got back home; he'd even be glad when he got back to school.

He had been so taken up with his own thoughts that he hadn't realized they were coming into Hexham station.

"I won't park, I'll just drop you, because I must get to see Dad."

Michael's voice was abrupt again and Mr. Jones said, "Of course, of course. And I don't know how to thank you. If I could only do something to repay your kindness, and your mother's."

For a moment there was a glimpse of the joker that Daniel had become acquainted with as Michael said, "Come up for a few days at shearing and then for a

month in the summer—that should clear the debt." Michael brought the truck to a stop.

As he lowered his head to get out, Mr. Jones said, "Right. Right. We just might do that. What do you say, Daniel?" But Daniel, who was already in the road, said nothing; he simply lifted his hand and returned Michael's salute.

It was almost a half hour later when they were sitting in the train for Newcastle that Mr. Jones said, "You know, I cannot remember a time that I've enjoyed more. We only met them around half-past three yesterday yet I feel it's years away and I seem to have known them all for a lifetime."

It was quite some seconds before Daniel replied slowly, "You didn't think it was odd that you never had the chance to say good-bye to Sally?"

"No, because she wasn't there. While you were upstairs her mother told me the neighboring farmer had called and picked her up to go and spend the day with them. They have four children between the ages of twelve and four."

"Mrs. Everton said that?" Daniel's face was screwed up.

"Yes, what's strange about that?"

"What's strange about that?" Daniel repeated each word slowly. "Only that Sally was in the house all the time; I saw her at the upper window just before I got into the car. And what's more, she had a busted face as if she had been in a fight. Now tell me that I imagined I heard screams in the night."

3

It was nearly seven weeks later when Mr. Jones got his car back. During this time there had been snowstorms like no one had ever remembered before. The car had lain at the side of the road for three weeks, and when it was finally towed to the garage so many things were found to be wrong with it that Mrs. Everton had informed him on the phone that the garage owner had suggested it would be better to let it go for scrap. But Mr. Jones wouldn't hear of this, and so four weeks later he picked up the car together with a very large bill.

The roads now were temporarily clear and so, being relatively near the farm, he made it his business to go and commiserate in person with Mrs. Everton on her loss, for her husband had died some three days previously.

Daniel had not accompanied him and for the first time he and his father had really had words bordering on what could be called a fight. Was he still harping on about those silly ideas? his father had demanded. And to this Daniel had come back with, "All right, if they are silly ideas then I must be going out of my head. Either I heard screams and saw her face or I didn't, and if I didn't and thought I did, then I must be going crazy." And to this his father, before going out and banging the door, had replied, "And that could be possible."

But later that evening when his father returned there was no anger in him; in fact his manner was placating. After saying, "Any tea kicking about?" he sat down at the kitchen table and, joining his hands on it, he looked at them as he said, "I'm sorry, Daniel, that I went for you about that business, because it seems that in parts you're right. Of course, I didn't hear any screaming and I didn't see the young lass before I left because, as I told you, her mother said she had gone to friends. But today when I saw her, although her face wasn't still swollen, there were definitely the signs that she'd had a cut lip. What's more, she had lost two front teeth and, by all accounts, she's going to the hospital in Newcastle for special fittings of some sort. Apparently her teeth are chalky, so her mother said, and false ones would have to be drilled into the gums or some such. Yet"—he lifted his head now and turned toward Daniel, who was about to hand him a cup of tea—"apart from the sorrow that they're feeling over the loss of the father, the three of them seemed close. It was Michael who insisted I stay and have something to eat. And he couldn't have been nicer to the lass. Just before I went to take my leave I saw them in the passageway: she was leaning against him and he was holding her tenderly. I can't make it out. But I'll tell you what I think: I think there may be somebody in the family stuck up in the attic.

You know this does sometimes happen when there's a relative not right in the head. They don't want them put in an asylum or some place of care, so they keep them hidden. Cases have come to light again and again."

Daniel now sat opposite his father and shook his head for a moment before saying, "I can't see it like that."

Mr. Jones sighed now as he remarked, "You remember he talked a lot, Michael did, that night we were there. It could have been a sort of cover-up, putting us at our ease. And then Mrs. Everton's lying to me about Sally's going to stay with friends. It's fishy. And you know, boy"—he smiled now across at Daniel—"I'm really sorry I went for you about the whole business. I've thought a lot about it on my way back and about the warm invitation we've got to visit anytime we like. Sally asked particularly when you were coming again. She even wanted to know why you hadn't come along with me today. I said you were working hard for your exams. But you know something? Since my visit and seeing that girl's face, which confirmed all you said, I've got a feeling that we should go back. I've never felt so curious about anything before. How do you feel about it?"

How did he feel about it? Frightened? No, not exactly frightened now. Curious then? Yes, perhaps; but not curious enough to make him want to spend another night there, and he voiced this: "I . . . I don't think I'd like to spend another night there, Dad."

"Well, I can assure you, if we ever should I'd determine to sleep light or give you the order to shake me awake with a kick or by any other appropriate method." He laughed now, and then on a more sober note added, "That fellow was there. His full name is Billy Combo. There's certainly no love lost between Michael and him."

"How does Mrs. Everton take him?"

"I really couldn't say. She's pleasant enough to him. I didn't stay long, but long enough to know that I would have one thing in common with Michael—I wouldn't be able to stand that little fellow. He's a slimy bloke. Well now, what do you say, after your next trip to Carlisle, we call in?"

Daniel hesitated for a long moment and then he said, "I'll leave it to you, Dad."

"All right then, we'll call in."

But Daniel didn't have a trip to Carlisle; he caught influenza after getting soaked through on the playing field. He was in bed for three weeks and when he got up he had to find the use of his legs, which to his dismay seemed to have grown inches longer. And it was during the second week of his convalescence and on a Friday afternoon that the Evertons paid a surprise visit.

Daniel opened the door to them and stood with his mouth slightly agape as he looked at the three smiling faces. It wasn't until Michael said in what appeared to be his characteristic way, "You going to leave us on the doorstep then?" that Daniel cried, "Come in. Come in. I'm . . . I'm just surprised, but I'm glad to see you."

"Well, you should look it another time." Michael laughed at him, and Mrs. Everton said, "Take no notice, Daniel. How are you now?"

"Oh, I'm fine."

"You've gotten taller still."

Daniel blushed as he looked down on Sally, saying, "Yes. I know. It's getting to be a worry."

"You should worry. I'd swap you any day." Michael

now lifted a bag onto the kitchen table and, pointing to it, Sally said, "We've brought you lots of things to fatten you up—eggs, butter and cream and a hock of bacon and . . ."

"Be quiet, Sally."

"It's very kind of you." Daniel was looking at Mrs. Everton but his mind was still on Sally, thinking how changed she seemed, perky, talkative. But there was still the scar on her lip, and as he looked at her again she squared her lips at him and dug her index finger at her teeth, saying, "I've got my new teeth today."

"Oh." He could find nothing more to say until Michael chipped in again as he looked at his mother, saying, "We always offer people a cup of tea when they visit us, don't we, Mom?"

"Oh, I'm sorry. Sit down. Sit down. Or . . . come into the sitting room."

"No, no"—Mrs. Everton waved her hand at him—"we'll sit here. But I could do with a cup of tea."

"You'll have it in two shakes."

As Daniel busied himself putting the kettle on he chatted, answering questions and asking one or two himself, the last one being as he handed the cups of tea around, "Who's looking after the farm?" he said.

After a short pause, Mary Everton answered, "Billy turned up last week—he does at times—and as Sally had to come into Newcastle I thought it was a good idea for a break and a chance to do some shopping."

Daniel noticed that Michael made no comment on this; in fact, presently he changed the subject by saying, "You'll have missed a lot of schooling and just at a bad time."

"Yes, but I've been working when I could. I take my

exams next week, and I have a feeling the number of passes will be zero."

"Well, that'll make a pair of us," said Michael. But his mother chipped in, saying, "You passed five exams, what are you talking about?"

"Yes, all in subjects that are no use to a farmer: Art, French, History, English Lit, Religious Knowledge, and although, on second thought, farmers have to rely on God, the weather He sends is never the right kind. Anyway, apart from calling in to see how you are, the main object of the visit is to see if you would like to come and spend part of your vacation with us. Of course there's a method in our madness, in mine at least: it's a busy time and I want another hand."

There was a moment of hesitation before Daniel replied, "Oh, thank you. Thank you very much. Yes, I'd like to come."

"What about your father?"

Daniel looked at Mrs. Everton now, saying, "Oh, he wouldn't mind me going. Anyway, it . . . it would give him a chance to come up on weekends too."

"A busman's holiday."

"Yes, doing gardening all day, you'd think he'd want a change from the country. But his main ambition in life is to have a cottage and a plot of land. I think he dreams about it. Well, you know what happened when we went to look at a particular cottage."

"Do you go to dances?"

The question caused all eyes to turn on Sally, and Daniel smiled ruefully as he said, "Not very often. I'm . . . I'm no good at dancing, even when you are doing your own thing. In fact"—he began to chuckle now—"I haven't been since a girl told me that I had legs like an octopus and they were all left ones and all over the place. I suppose it's one of the penalties of being lanky."

Amid the laughter he now looked at Sally and asked her, "Do you go?"

"No"—her face had a solemn look as she added—"but I see them on television."

"We are . . . we are too far away from the town," her mother put in quickly now Then, gathering up her handbag, she said, "Well, we'll have to be on our way—it's a longish ride back. I'm sorry we can't stay till your father gets in, but tell him we'll look forward to seeing him and that I hope he'll agree to your spending some of your vacation with us."

As they were about to take their departure, Sally caused some consternation by looking up at Daniel and saying, "Will you take me to a dance sometime?"

Before Daniel had time to answer, Michael gave his sister a push through the open front door and onto the pavement, almost barking at her, "Go on, get out, or I'll dance you, you brazen hussy." And Mrs. Everton, shaking her head, now said, "It was different in my day; you waited until you were asked."

There was no need for him to give any reply to this, for Michael was bundling his mother and Sally into the Land-Rover.

The next minute they were off. Daniel looked after them for a few moments, then went inside and closed the door.

He stood with his back to it, thinking. He was going to spend his summer vacation on a farm; he should feel excited. Well, was he? He didn't really know because there was something, still that something troubling him, and strangely, unlike his father, he didn't want to get to the bottom of it. Perhaps he was a coward in more ways than one, afraid to be caught up in other people's lives. The self-criticism was disturbing. It made him feel low, of no account.

Slowly he went into the kitchen and began to empty the bag of food, and when it was arrayed on the table he stood looking down on it, muttering, "They're kind. That's one thing about them, they're kind."

4

The first week of the summer vacation was over, and Daniel had enjoyed the five days he had already spent on the farm. Up to a point, that is, and the point that set the query was the name Combo.

Combo, he knew, didn't like him and he certainly didn't like Combo. He felt that his own dislike of the man almost equaled Michael's, yet at the present time Michael, he knew, was glad of Combo's services, for he was an experienced farmhand whereas Daniel himself was, as Michael had laughingly put it, an overanxious bungler. He could feed the chickens. Well, anyone could feed chickens. He could feed the pigs. Again, anyone could feed the pigs. And he could muck the latter out. But it wasn't everybody who jumped at that chance.

And now today with the cows. There were not enough of them to warrant the expense of milking machinery so the milking was done by hand. And his efforts in this were causing hilarious hoots from Sally, laughter from her mother, and the usual chipping from Michael. But Billy Combo's reactions to Daniel's efforts were a shrug and the words: "What do you expect from a woolly-headed, gangling townie?"

Daniel's innate disinclination to start a quarrel that might end in physical blows for one rare moment deserted him and he had made to follow the man out of the cow barns. But Mrs. Everton laid her hand gently on his arm and, shaking her head, said, "No, no, please. He . . . he doesn't mean half he says." Nevertheless, she herself followed the man outside and Daniel saw her through the open door of the barns talking to Combo. But it didn't look from this distance as if she were reprimanding him, rather that she were pleading with him, for her hands were joined together at her waist and the expression on her face indicated anything but harshness. Sally too was looking toward her mother, and presently she said, "I wonder how he would have stood up to you if you had gone for him?" But before he had time to make any reply whatever, Michael spoke from where he was sitting on a small stool to the side of a cow. "He wouldn't have only stood up to you, he would have savaged you. He's vicious. I've seen him in a fight." Then he added, more to himself as he leaned his head against the cow's side, "But one of these days he'll get a surprise, and I hope I live long enough to give it to him."

It was Friday morning when he received the letter from his mother. He had written and made excuses for not visiting her, saying he had been invited to spend the vacation on the Evertons' farm. Her reply was anything but pleasant. It was his duty, she said, to come and see her, and if he couldn't spare the time, then she would come and see him. After all, he was her son and he should remind his father that he was bound by the court ruling until he himself was sixteen, which was still three months away. What attitude he would take then toward her she would leave to his conscience and his sense of duty, she said, which she feared wouldn't be encouraged in him if he listened to his father.

He read the letter at the breakfast table and Mrs. Everton, noticing his face, said, "Bad news, Daniel?" And to this he replied, "It's how you look at it, Mrs. Everton. It's from me mother. She's playing war with me because I haven't been to see her over the last six weeks."

"Didn't she know you hadn't been well?"

"Yes, yes, but then she doesn't lay much stock on illness, especially colds. She never had a cold—she was never ill, not that I can remember."

"She's a very lucky woman then. . . . Don't you want to go and see her?"

He hung his head for a moment, aware that the eyes of both Michael and Sally were on him. Then his chin jerking upward, he answered truthfully, "Not very much. I . . . I don't like her new husband. To my mind the only thing he's got is money."

"Well, that isn't a bad thing."

Daniel looked steadily at Michael now and, although he knew Michael was joking, he answered him soberly, saying, "Well, it isn't always good. The more you get, the more you want. That's how Dad's always seen it, and I think I go along with him: you can't be happy on just money."

"Some people manage." Michael rose from the table now. "And if you come across anybody who wants to get rid of any, let me know, will you? Or have you got any yourself stacked away that you don't want?"

"Yes. Yes." Daniel nodded at him, joining in with Michael's mood. "I've got seven pounds fifty pence in the savings bank and I've got eight pounds upstairs to carry me over the vacation."

"Good. Good. We'll go into Hexham tonight and blow that."

"Will you?" Sally bounced up from her chair, adding now, "Oh! Michael, may I come?"

"Don't be silly"—her mother flapped her hands at her—"he was only joking. And come and get these things cleared away. But wait, before that, go to the bottom of the coach house stairs and call Billy. By the look of things he's sleeping off his night out."

"I'll go."

"No." Mrs. Everton moved quickly toward her son, adding now, "I want no trouble, Michael. For the rest of the time he's here, let things be."

"How long will that be?"

"Well, that depends on you. It was your suggestion that the bottom field should be cleared of stones and you should try tilling."

"I could do it meself, well, with the help of Daniel here. He's got another four weeks at least, that's if he wants to stay." He now glanced toward Daniel and Daniel, with a wry smile, answered, "I'll stay as long as you let me, outdo me welcome likely in the end." He was looking at Mary

Everton, but she made no direct answer. Turning to her son again, she said, "I'll tell him he'll be finished at the end of next week. I'll put it to him that we can't afford to pay him."

"Put it any way you like, but get him out of my hair, Mom." Michael had turned about and was walking toward the door, and Daniel made haste to follow him. But he hesitated just long enough at the door to hear Sally say to her mother, "I can never understand, Mom, why Dad made a friend of that man: Dad was nice, Combo's awful."

Yes, why had Mr. Everton made a friend of a man like Combo? He himself had never met the farmer, but going by everyone's opinion, he had been a very nice man, a good man, and so, as Sally had said, why did he take up with someone like Combo?

Twenty-four hours later Daniel was given the reason.

5

Saturday morning everybody was up early and busy about his own particular task, for there was a fête on over the hills and they were all hoping to attend in the afternoon. Michael was going to enter the hill race and his mother had already made a Dundee cake and scones, with which she hoped to compete against the other farmers' wives. Sally had done a tapestry square for a stool. This had already been sent in and in her mother's opinion stood a good chance in the County Craft Class for the under-fourteens. The only one who didn't want to go to the fair was Combo. A lot of country know-it-alls showing how little they knew, had been his verdict of the show at breakfast. Half of them, he said, knew nothing about sheep, being unable to tell wet rot from dry rot. Apparently, by the look on his face he had expected a laugh at this, but when none was forthcoming he added with a growl, "Aye well, I could buy them at one end of the field and sell them at t'other, the lot of 'em. And not only sheep either."

Daniel understood from a remark Mrs. Everton had made that Combo was indeed very knowledgeable where sheep were concerned, and he himself had noticed that when the man went among the sheep they didn't scatter as when he himself went into the fields. But knowledge of sheep or no knowledge of sheep, he was, in Daniel's opinion, a loud-mouthed, ignorant man.

He was working on the platform in the barn and was just about to pull a bundle of hay from the far corner when he heard Combo's voice. Apparently he was speaking to Mrs. Everton, who must have just come into the barn, and he had followed her, because the place had been empty a moment ago.

Combo's voice was low but his words came distinctly to Daniel: "You didn't mean what you said, did you, Mary?"

"I'm afraid I did, Billy," Mrs. Everton replied.

"There's still a lot to do."

"Be that as it may, Billy, as I've told you, I . . . I can't afford to keep you on."

"That for a tale. You know I'd work for nothing just to be here, you know that full well. I'm going to tell you something, Mary. You've . . . you've changed since John went. Me welcome's not so warm. You used to be glad to see me at one time."

"I was never . . ." Mrs. Everton's voice trailed away as if she regretted what she was about to say.

Daniel straightened his back but he made no move to

go toward the end of the platform and let his presence be known; and now Combo's voice came to him, harsh-sounding: "You were going to say you were never glad to see me, was that it?"

"You were John's friend so I made you welcome."

"Ho! ho! Mary, come off it. And don't take that line with me. All right, you know and I know why I was made welcome by John."

"Billy"—there was a plea in Mrs. Everton's voice now—"I want no trouble. I've had enough. Please do as I ask—leave us at the end of next week. You can come again later."

There was a pause now before Combo replied, "Come again later, you say. That's maybe because somebody's getting to be a big boy now and throwing his weight about. It's a wonder it wasn't he himself who told me to be gettin' on me way and not you. But give him another year and the hills won't hold him."

"Billy, please. Look, do as I ask, go on a round—there's plenty work to be had here and there—then . . . then you can come back for the winter."

There was another silence. Daniel stood with his head to the side, his ears strained, and for a moment he thought they must both have gone quietly from the barn, until Combo's voice came again, saying, "What if I decide to stay, permanently like? I've thought about it a lot, even before John went. But now I could stay on different terms. You want a man here, Mary, not just a young kid, or a traveling hand, but a man permanently. How about it?"

Mrs. Everton's voice hardly reached Daniel for her words seemed to be caught in her breath as she said, "What do you mean?"

"You know full well what I mean. I've always had a fancy for you. You're bound to know that too, an' you wouldn't be making such a bad bargain. I've got me health, not like John, God rest him, and there's nothing I don't know about running a farm. If I hadn't been such a blasted fool I would have had me own long afore now."

When Daniel heard Mrs. Everton's voice, no longer a whisper but a strangled yell as she cried, "Let me go! Let me go! Do you hear?" it brought him as if out of a trance and springing toward the edge of the platform; but there he halted, for Michael had appeared in the barn doorway and the voice with which he spoke was not that of a youth but came deep-bellied as if from a man of stature.

"Take your hands off my mother."

Daniel, standing stiffly on the edge of the platform, watched Combo swing around. Then it seemed as if in a flash Michael and he met with fists flailing. But Michael, as young and strong as he was, was no match for the mature Combo. Such was his strength born of anger, however, that he delivered two blows to Combo's face before he found himself dashed against the timbers of the barn. Then Combo, reaching out, grabbed up a pitchfork and, standing over him, yelled down at him between gasps, "For two pins I'd ram this into your upstart face. Who do you think you are, anyway? Well, I'm gonna tell you who you are. I'm gonna give you the answer to your words. Take your hands off my mother, you said. Well, for your information, Mr. Big-Head, you've got no mother. She's as much your mother as she is mine. You don't belong to anybody. Never did. So what do you think of yourself now, Mr. Would-Be-Farmer?"

From where Daniel was standing at the bottom of the

ladder he could see the look on Michael's face, the eyes and mouth stretched wide as if he were viewing something amazing, horrifyingly amazing. And then he watched him look toward where Mrs. Everton was standing, her head bowed, one hand covering her eyes while with the other she supported herself against the stanchion of the barn. He did not at this moment stop to consider that he hated fighting, that he was afraid of fights, and that at bottom he was a coward and scared of being hurt both physically and mentally, for now he seemed to take a flying leap as if he were practicing a rugby tackle. When he landed on Combo's back, the surprise attack made the man loosen his hold on the pitchfork. But within seconds Daniel felt himself falling backward, and the impact of his back hitting the floor and the body on top of him momentarily stunned him. He still managed to retain his hold on Combo's neck, but the man must have been used to combat of all kinds for with a deft movement he sprang Daniel's grip, and the next minute Daniel found himself being jabbed by Combo's knees and pummeled by his fists. Though he struck out blindly and once felt the impact of his own fist against Combo's mouth, he was definitely aware that the man was too much for him and that he was being knocked senseless.

Then like an answer to the unconscious prayer that was tearing around in his head, crying, "Oh, dear God! Oh, dear God!" Combo's body was torn from him, and he saw him, as if through a haze, rising upward. At the same time he knew something serious was happening to him. Perhaps it was death, for vaguely he knew his father was fighting his battle for him, and the battle for Michael, and the battle for Mrs. Everton, and the battle for Sally . . .

for that was her voice screaming, and then the great blackness overwhelmed him and he sank into it.

His face was wet; he thought for a moment he was swimming underwater but he couldn't open his eyes, not even when he heard a voice saying, "It's all right, he's coming round. Don't worry now, don't worry. He'll be all right."

"Oh, I'm sorry. I'm sorry."

That was Mrs. Everton speaking, and he wondered what it was she was sorry about? And when his father spoke he knew it was himself she was sorry for, for his father was saying, "Likely done him the world of good, although I never thought to see him go for anybody like he did for that individual. He's never been the fighting kind really, something like meself."

"Well, if you're not the fighting kind, you certainly showed up to some advantage today. I . . . I don't know what would have happened if you hadn't come on the scene."

"Oh, Michael would have finished him off likely. Where is he, by the way."

The silence that followed was so long that Daniel tried to open his eyes. But the effort was tiring, so he kept them closed. And then he heard Mrs. Everton saying in a low sad voice, "He's likely walking the hills; he . . . he got a shock."

"A shock? You mean because he was knocked out?"

"No, not that kind of a shock." There was another pause before she went on, "You see, he had just learned that he . . . he was adopted. He's not really my son."

Now Daniel opened his eyes and looked upward.

Neither his father nor Mrs. Everton were paying him any attention, but were looking at each other as Mrs. Everton said, "I thought we'd never have any children. We . . . we lived in Devon at the time. We had a small farm there, nothing much. There was a cottage on the land. It had been occupied for years by a family called Bingham. There was only the old granny left and one day her granddaughter turned up. She was only eighteen and she herself was an orphan and had been brought up for most of her life in a home. But there she was on the point of giving birth. Within two days of her arrival Michael was born. I helped to bring him into the world, so he . . . he seemed mine right from the start. The grandmother couldn't look after the child and the mother didn't want it. She was young, you see. So when we said we'd love to adopt it she was only too pleased. And . . . and that's the story."

"Then he's got a mother somewhere?"

"No, I'm glad to say he hasn't. She died three years later. She was drowned, of all things. She was no swimmer and she got caught in a current. Strangely, she died before her granny did. Anyway, we moved here when Michael was just on four and, stranger still, I was then carrying Sally. And here we've lived ever since as one family."

"But . . . but excuse me asking, how does Combo come into this?"

Daniel watched Mrs. Everton now turn to the bowl of water that was standing on the table and wring out another cloth while saying, "When drink's in, sense is out. John had taken too much one night at a reunion meeting, and it was there he met up with Combo, whom surprisingly he had been friends with while they were doing their National Service. I say surprisingly because no two men could be more like chalk and cheese than my husband and that man. Anyway, John told him the circumstances of Michael's birth. The next day he wouldn't have realized he had done it, but Combo made sure he let him know. From then Combo has been a regular visitor, and John always seemed glad of his help. Of course I used to say there was no accounting for tastes, but John always seemed to like the fellow; he would make excuses for him, saying he was a rough diamond and that he had a heart of gold, et cetera. Well, he's gone now. And so has Michael, for in a way I . . . I think Michael will never forgive me: the way he looked at me when he went out of the barn, it was as if he hated me."

"No. No. It would just be the shock. Sort of finding out you don't belong, I mean by birth. It must be a shock, not only when you're young but at any age."

"Oh, you're awake. How are you feeling?" Mrs. Everton was bending over him.

Daniel raised himself on his elbow on the couch, then, smiling weakly, answered, "As . . . as if I'd had me brains knocked out."

"Well, it wasn't his fault that you didn't." It was his father standing over him now. "Can't leave you a minute but you get into a scrap. You'll find yourself behind bars if you keep this up."

"Oh, Dad"—Daniel drooped his head—"don't be funny. I don't feel like laughing."

"No, I don't suppose you do. Come on, sit up and have a cup of tea. Oh, here's Sally." Mr. Jones smiled toward the young girl as she came slowly into the room and he watched her look toward her mother as she said sadly, "I can't see him anywhere, Mom."

"Don't worry; he'll be back shortly."

"The fair'll be off now, won't it?" There was a keen note of disappointment in the young girl's voice and her mother, taking the kettle off the stove and making the tea, said, "We'll see. We'll see."

Sally was now standing in front of Daniel, and when she put her hand out and tentatively touched his cheekbone with her finger he felt the color flushing over his face. And when she said, "Does it hurt?" he answered, "No, not yet."

"Your eye will be black tomorrow."

"Thanks. Thanks very much." He smiled weakly at her. And now she smiled back at him, saying, "Well, it will; it's half closed already."

"Sally!" Her mother's tone was stern. "When will you learn to be tactful?"

"I was only saying . . ."

"Yes, I know you were only saying, but you're saying the wrong thing."

"Oh, I don't know."

Because of the look on Sally's face, Daniel felt forced to take her part. " 'Tis the right thing she's saying," he said; "it will be black tomorrow with shades of blue and yellow. I've seen them." He turned to his father now, adding, "Saturday night in the city you see some beauties, don't you, Dad?"

"You do indeed. And we must take a picture of yours and preserve it, because, as Sally says, it'll be black tomorrow and, to my mind, big enough to get into the Guinness Book of World Records."

At this Sally gave a high-pitched laugh, then clamped her hands over her mouth and, turning to her mother, said, "I'm sorry."

"Why be sorry for laughing?" Mrs. Everton was carrying a tray to the table, and after she laid it down she put out her hand and gently patted her daughter's cheek. Sally's reaction to this was to clutch at her mother's hand and to hold it tightly against her face for a moment.

The scene was slightly embarrassing for Daniel, and after glancing at his father, who was smiling quietly, he looked away. Then all of a sudden he was enveloped in a feeling of faintness again, and this brought a strong admonition from within as he told himself, "Don't pass out again. You've only got a black eye."

"Would you like to go and lie down for a while, Daniel?"

"Take him up, Peter, will you?"

She had called his father Peter. How long had she been doing that? And he was still pondering on this question when ten minutes later he fell asleep.

He woke up once and drank a bowl of soup that Sally had brought up on a tray. He remembered that she had sat watching him drink it, but he didn't remember her taking the tray away.

The next time he woke up a strange man was bending over him saying, "Slightly concussed. Just let him sleep; he'll be all right in a day or two. If his heart's anything to go by he's as strong as a horse."

Life had turned funny—he was sleeping it away. He wanted to wake up and to stay awake.

When he finally woke up, the bedside lamp was lit and sitting looking at him was Michael.

He stared at him for a moment before saying, "What time is it?"

"Oh, somewhere around nine, I think."

"Have I been asleep all day?"

"Most part of it."

"What happened? Was it my eye?"

"Don't talk crazy; you don't sleep through a black eye. You've got a concussion. You can't hit a stone floor with your head and expect it to bounce."

"Is that what happened?"

"That's what happened."

Why had he hit the stone floor with his head? He closed his eyes again and as he did so the reason came flooding back. Now, looking at Michael once more, he asked him, "You all right?"

"Yes, I'm all right."

"I'm sorry."

"What you sorry about?"

"Well"—he moved his head slowly on the pillow—"about what happened: Combo going for your mother and . . ."

"What do you mean, and . . . ? Well, go on, finish. You're sorry, not only for Combo going for . . . my mother, but for the fact that I learned that she isn't my mother. That's it, isn't it?"

There was a long pause before Daniel said, "You're a funny guy."

"It's not the first time I've heard that."

"I . . . I didn't mean it nasty like. I didn't mean it funny ha! ha! either."

"What exactly did you mean then?"

Daniel drew in a long breath, settled his head on the pillow, and looked away from Michael before he said, "I don't really know, except that you . . . well, you seem two or three different people at different times."

"And I don't know which one is me?"

The words were so sad sounding, and Daniel, looking at Michael again, said, "Your mother . . . and I mean your mother, is a lovely woman and I can tell you this: I've envied you her more than once since I first came here. . . . My mother . . . well, she wasn't like a mother at all, not in the way yours is, because Mrs. Everton . . . your mom, thinks about everybody else but herself. Mine never seemed to think much about me until she left home, and not even then, not until the divorce came through and she married again. And now she insists on her legal rights, so called, that I spend some time with her every week. It used to be every Saturday until she went to live in Carlisle. Now it's a weekend once a month, but she insists I make up the time during school vacation. That Saturday you came upon us on the road followed one such do that had been cut short because I phoned Dad and told him if he didn't come and get me I'd start walking back home."

"Don't you like her, I mean at all?"

Daniel thought for a long moment before he said, "Not very much now. Yet at one time I seemed to be crazy about her. That was because I wanted her to like me. Well"—he blinked rapidly—"more than like me." He turned his head to the side now and looked at Michael as he ended, "Be like your mother, caring. All mine cared about was herself and clothes and vacations abroad. She went on vacations abroad by herself."

"She did?"

"Yes, because Dad isn't for that kind of vacation; he likes rivers, canals. One year when she was off on her own he took me for a week on a canal. I . . . I should have enjoyed it but all the time I was thinking about her and wishing I was with her. And when she came back she seemed to be in a temper for weeks. The fact is, she didn't like Dad being content to be a gardener."

"What's the man she's got now?"

"Oh, he's in big business. He's got a flat in Edinburgh besides this house in Carlisle." He now grinned painfully at Michael as he said, "It was rotten of me, I know, but that particular Saturday morning before I left, I looked around their lounge—that's what she called it. Everything was shiny, brassy, new, not used like. We had just been going at it, her and me, and he had come in and started to play the new daddy and I turned to Mom and said, 'It's a good thing Granda's dead, isn't it, because if he came here he'd have nowhere to spit.' I know she could have killed me."

Daniel now laughed, then held his aching head for a moment before adding, "Me granda Smith was an awful old man. He hated washing. Mom left home when she was young. She wouldn't own him or me granny. But he used to present himself at the front door every now and again. Dad and he got on well together. Dad always swore that Granda put on his worst side just to vex her; he said behind it all he was an intelligent man but a bit of a rebel."

"I think I might have liked him, that granda of yours. We would likely have gotten on well together." There was a smile in Michael's eyes now and Daniel said, "Yes, I think you're right. He used to have some funny sayings; he used to say, it isn't how you're born or if you're born to the blue, but how you die and where you're going to."

Solemn-faced, they stared at each other through the pink glow of the bedside lamp. Then Daniel said softly, "Like me granda said, 'tisn't how you're born. And taking all in all, from what I've seen I think you're lucky. And I can tell you this: I . . . I wouldn't mind where I came from or who borned me—eeh! that's grammar if you like—if I was in your shoes. I'd change places with you anytime 'coz—" he swallowed deeply now and there was a restriction in his throat for a moment before he could finish, saying, "you don't know what it's like not to have a mother, what I mean is, to have one and know that she doesn't care, that you don't come first, not even second or third with her. It's an awful feeling. What I'm meaning to say is—"

He stopped abruptly as he watched Michael rise to his feet. He watched him push the chair back against the wall, then come and stand close to the bed and make a feint gesture as if to punch him as he said, "You've made your point, Socrates, you've made your point. Now go to sleep again. Good night."

Michael had reached the door before Daniel said, quietly, "Good night." Then again, "Good night, Michael."

All of a sudden he felt happy, relaxed, and tired, so tired, he felt he could sleep forever. . . . Well, not forever, for life surprisingly suddenly promised to be good.

6

The following morning Daniel woke to see his father sitting by his bedside, and again he asked, "What time is it?"

"About quarter to ten."

"Good gracious!" He made to get up but his father's hand pressed him back into the pillows. "Lie still," he said.

"But I'm feeling all right, Dad."

"Yes, no doubt, until you stand on your feet. You've got to stay there today."

Daniel relaxed, his head dropping deep into the pillow. He put his hand to his face. It was sore. He could feel his eyes swollen. He must look a mess. He said so: "Do I look awful, Dad?"

"Well, all I can say is"—his father now grinned at him—

"you were never any beauty and that eye doesn't improve things."

"You're a comfort." He tried to smile, but was then surprised to see the expression that was now on his father's face. It had suddenly become serious; it was the look that he wore when he was troubled about something.

"Anything wrong, Dad?" he asked.

"I don't know."

"What do you mean by that?"

"Well"—his father leaned toward him now and in a low voice said, "You were right that time about the screaming."

Daniel said nothing, he just continued to look at his father. And Mr. Jones went on, "You know me of old, once my head touches the pillow, I'm off, but last night I was a bit worried about you and I lay awake—well, just dozing—when I heard it. It . . . it brought me upright but it wasn't a scream."

"Then what was it?"

Mr. Jones looked to the side, then gently moved his fingers through his hair before he said, "I can't describe it. I've told myself several times I must have been dreaming and I would have thought so if it hadn't been for what you heard. No, it wasn't a scream, it was more like a dull, strangled cry, and it came from"—he jerked his head up toward the ceiling—"but not from right above as you said it did; it seemed to come from the far end of the house somehow. And you know, I would have thought I had imagined it even then until I heard movement outside the door there." Again he jerked his head, but sideways now. "Well, what do you make of it?"

"If I could tell you that, the mystery would be solved. I

only feel that whoever's up there, and definitely it's somebody, they are in pain or—" he now looked down toward where his hands were resting on his knees and ended—"demented."

There was silence for a time until Daniel said, "Remember Sally's face, but she's not demented."

"No, she certainly isn't. But I've been thinking: whoever is up there could have attacked her."

"Yes"—Daniel nodded to himself—"yes, that could be, Dad. But I've been here over a week and I've never seen Mrs. Everton take any food out of the kitchen, like a tray or anything, and we've all sat down to the meal together."

"Oh, that signifies nothing. You would have been outside most of the day, I should imagine, and there're ways and means of getting food to somebody on the quiet. Anyway, they are all of the same mind about whoever's up there, that's evident, for they're not letting on in any way. You've heard nothing more during the week you've been here, nor seen anything odd like?"

"No; no, Dad, except . . . well, there's a wooden staircase leading up to a door at the far end of the house. I asked Sally where it led to, and she said, oh, it was just another way into the attics. When I come to think of it she did seem a bit offhand about it and, as she often does, she went on chattering about something else."

"Well"—Mr. Jones rose to his feet—"I expect it'll come to light one day; I can't imagine they can keep a thing like that secret forever. There could, I suppose, be some simple explanation."

"Simple? I wouldn't say that the scream I heard came from something you could call simple. No, I wouldn't."

"Well, anyway, we'll have to wait and see. I'll go down

now and get your breakfast."

As his father went toward the door, Daniel asked, "How's Michael this morning?"

"Quiet." His father turned and nodded toward him. "But then he would be: he's had a bit of a shock. But he'll get over it when he realizes how fortunate he's been, having a woman like Mary for a mother."

There it was again, his dad calling Mrs. Everton Mary. It was odd somehow and it made him feel uneasy; he immediately thought of his mother. He must write to her and tell her not to come here, as in her last letter she had threatened to do. Somehow he felt she wouldn't like Mrs. Everton and so would try under some pretext to get him away.

As he settled down on the pillow once more he remembered hearing Mrs. Everton call his dad Peter, and he thought: They haven't known each other five minutes.

Daniel came downstairs on Monday morning in spite of Mrs. Everton's insistence that he should stay in bed until the doctor had another look at him; but knowing the work that had to be done, he felt that he was imposing by lying in bed and having meals carried up to him. If, as she said, he must rest, then he could do so down in the kitchen.

They were just finishing breakfast when a tap came on the back door, and before Michael had time to rise from the table it was opened, which made him swing quickly in his chair. Then he said, "Oh, hello there, Ralph."

"Sorry to interrupt you at your meal, Mary."

"That's all right, Ralph. Come and sit down and have a cup of tea."

"No, thanks. I've already had a mug with Arthur Beaconsfield, here, and another of Flo Newberry's coffee, and you know what that's like—you can stick a knife in it."

"Anything wrong, Ralph?" Michael had now risen to his feet, a piece of toast in one hand and a cup in the other.

"Yes, I should say there is, Michael. Peter lost seven sheep last night."

"No!" Michael put the cup down on the table, then laid his slice of toast on the plate, and he repeated, "Seven?"

"Aye, seven. Clean as a whistle, not a sign of wool, blood, or anything. When three weeks ago they took those half dozen from Maitland's, they skinned the beggars. Remember this time last year? There were six cases in a fortnight, then nothing. It's funny; it's got me puzzled. If it was a local gang, surely they would have gone for the young lambs; they would have brought more on the market. Speaking of markets, Peter had brought fifty down and they were in the home field."

"That's close to the house."

Mr. Threadgill looked at Mrs. Everton as he said, "Aye, couldn't be much closer; the field runs up to the back garden wall, and their garden's no wider than a potato patch."

"Couldn't have jumped the wall? He had trouble with an old ewe playing leader last year, hadn't he?"

Mr. Threadgill nodded at Michael, saying, "Yes, he had. She was a terror. She would push her way through barbed wire, that one, and all the others would follow her. But no, he's had the walls reinforced; I gave him a hand meself. More so, he's had sloping stakes put round this particular field that reach a good three feet above the wall and these are wired. No, whoever handled this latest raid walked in the gate and took his choice. Anyway, Michael, I thought I'd better warn you. Have you got any ready for the market on Tuesday?"

"No, not this week. Anyway it looks as though there'll be so many in that the prices are nearly sure to drop."

"They won't drop on mine." The big man jerked his chin upward. "I'll bring them back home first. Not after the winter we've had and all the work to keep them alive. Oh no. Wouldn't you, Mary, bring them back rather than lose on them?"

"Yes, yes, I would, Ralph."

"Well, remember that when you take yours in next week; don't let them get away with it. Well, I'm off." He looked at Michael now. "Keep your eyes open, both of them wide."

"I will that." As Michael walked toward the door with him, Mr. Threadgill said, "If it isn't one thing, it's another: damned idiots of townies letting their dogs off the leads to have a run. Boy! Nick Potter's never gotten over that business last month: nine of them with their throats torn. He said Jane cried for two solid days. All through that terrible weather she had seen to those lambs; she helped them to survive. If they had been left alone one after the other would have died, and then there they were, savaged. She knew them personally like children. You know what?" He now turned around and looked down the room toward Mary, saying bitterly, "We have the authority to shoot dogs that worry sheep but it isn't animals that should be shot, it's their owners."

Daniel was thinking at this moment that there were many sides to this farm life that he knew nothing about, had never imagined, and his mind was just registering the fact that the man had left, having completely ignored him, when Mr. Threadgill put his head around the door again and, speaking directly to him now, said, "Heard about the job you did on Combo, young fellow. And none too soon. Nasty piece of work that: too big in the mouth and too small in the brain. You've got a nice shiner there."

Before Daniel could reply, the head was withdrawn and Sally was saying, "He's a nice man. He's going to lend me a pony next year to learn to ride, isn't he, Mom?"

"Yes, yes."

Daniel noticed that Mrs. Everton's voice had an impatient, sharp note to it, and when Sally, suddenly swinging around in her chair, cried loudly, "Well, he is! And I am, I am," her mother stood looking at her for a moment, then in a quiet voice replied, "All right, he is, and you are. So now finish your breakfast."

Sally stared at her mother for a full minute before obeying her, and Daniel thought that this little scene should have explained something to him. But what? He couldn't probe at the moment; he could hardly think for his head was aching so.

As he rose from the table he mused that farms were supposed to be tranquil places where people lived in peace, but he was finding they weren't either tranquil or peaceful; they were places where things were always happening.

Looking back to his life in town in contrast, nothing seemed to have happened there, whereas here hardly an hour went by but something was afoot, and hardly a day passed without an emergency. He didn't know whether he would like to live his entire life on a farm, sort of make it his home . . . But why was he thinking this way? He had no reason to choose; he was merely on vacation.

On Tuesday he drove into the Hexham cattle market with Michael. Michael had nothing to sell; he just wanted to study the prices. The scene was such as Daniel had never witnessed before and for the first time he experienced the emotion of compassion. He didn't put that name to it, he only knew that the bobbing heads of hundreds of sheep pressed close together affected him, and that he felt sorry for a cow being prodded around a small ring. When a ram tried to jump the barrier and knocked several people over, his sympathies were with the ram.

It wasn't until they were on their way home that Michael remarked tersely, "You didn't enjoy the market?"

"No, not really."

"Why?"

"Well, I . . . I suppose you being brought up in the country, you . . . you wouldn't understand. It's a daily occurrence for you to see animals herded together."

"They're used to being herded together."

"And pushed around like they were and prodded with sticks?"

"The prodding they get would be the equivalent to a tap with a finger to you. And anyway there are R.S.P.C.A. men on the watch all the time for cruelty. There was no cruelty there."

"Do you think they knew they were going to die?"

"What!" The Rover swerved slightly and Michael gave a short laugh as he said, "Most of those you saw today were going back into the fields to breed next year's calves."

"Really?"

"Yes. As for those who go to the slaughterhouse . . . you like lamb, don't you?"

"I did."

"Oh, you did. Well, the next time a slice of roast lamb is put down in front of you, stick to your principles—don't eat it; nobody's forcing you. Anyway, what are you going on about? There's more care and attention given to animals today than to humans in many places, and if you want to feel sorry for animals, really sorry for animals, go abroad. If you were sorry for what you saw today, you'll spend the rest of your life howling your eyes out."

"You've seen animals abroad?"

"Aye, I have, first when I went with the school tour years ago and then eighteen months ago I went to North Africa for a month."

They drove in silence for some time until Michael spoke again. "You know," he said, "I don't think you'll take to country life, farm life, and as I seem to view things, that's going to be awkward, at least for you."

"What do you mean?"

Again it was some seconds before Michael replied. He had swung the Land-Rover from the main road onto the side road that led to the farm before he said, "Well, if you don't know what I'm getting at, I'm not going to enlighten you. Time'll tell, that's all. But what I think is, instead of being concerned about animals, you should turn your attention to humans and try to fathom their behavior and short memories. Or—" he now sighed as he ended—"perhaps it's their needs that I know nothing about as yet."

Daniel looked at his companion in silence. He was driving the Land-Rover at a breakneck speed now over the rough road. He certainly was a funny fellow, odd. He couldn't fathom him, let alone any other humans. But there must be something behind his cryptic remark. . . .

At the farm he found a letter awaiting him from his mother. He read it standing in the kitchen and Mrs. Everton, entering the room with Sally, both carrying bowls of strawberries, stopped and asked quietly, "Bad news, Daniel?"

He looked up from the letter saying, "It's how you look at it, Mrs. Everton. Me mom says she's coming on Saturday . . . here. She's determined I'm to go back with her."

Mrs. Everton put the bowl of strawberries down on the table before turning to Daniel and saying, "Well, if she wants you to go and stay with her then you must."

"No must about it, Mrs. Everton. I'm not going."

Mrs. Everton now motioned to Sally to bring her a fancy dish from the delft rack, and as she began sorting out the strawberries into it she said, "I understand she has some legal claim over you until you are sixteen. When will that be?"

"October."

"Well, that isn't so far away; surely you could comply with her wishes until then. It's understandable that she wants to see you."

"If she wanted to see me so badly she shouldn't have left me, or Dad."

"Oh, people's reactions can't be explained away as simply as that, Daniel. In many cases you never value anything till you have lost it, and perhaps that's what's happening to your mother now."

"She's got another husband; that should satisfy her."

"Yes, you would think it would, but it doesn't always work out that way."

"She wanted a better house and a big car and things like that, and now that she's got them, why can't she be satisfied? She's got the best end of the deal, because she left Dad in a hole."

"Oh, I wouldn't say she's got the best end of the deal. Big houses and cars are not enough to fill some wants in people's lives, and I don't really think you'll understand that, Daniel, until you're much older."

"I'm not a kid." For a moment he forgot to whom he was talking. When Mrs. Everton turned around and smiled at him gently, he bowed his head and said, "I'm . . . I'm sorry."

"Nothing to be sorry for Daniel. And I know you're not a kid. You look much older than your years and your height adds to this. But there are some things that one can't experience, especially in the teenage years; in fact no one would wish them to have such experiences. These years in youth are for learning how to live; they are not easy years. You'll likely look back later and find them the hardest in your life. I myself wouldn't want to live through my teens again because I see now I had so many false values. I felt I was right in most things I said, and believe it or not"—she smiled widely at him now—"although I might appear to you as a quiet sort of woman, in my teens I was a bit of a firebrand. I'll tell you something." She now glanced at Sally as she said, "And you don't know this, but my father locked me in my room once for two days. He had forbidden me to see a certain boy and I was determined to see this young man. But I must admit he wasn't all that young, being twelve years older than me. I was seventeen at the time, and if I could have gotten out I would have run off with him. And I know now my life would have been ruined, because, now listen—" she divided her glance between Daniel and her daughter now—"he had been twice married and his second wife, to whom he was still married, lived in Bolton. My father, when he pushed me into the bedroom, slapped my ears for me and I thought I'd never forgive him. A week later I laid my head on his chest and cried my eyes out. . . . Here, put some cream on these strawberries," she said, pushing a bowl of the fruit along the table toward Daniel. Slowly now he folded up the letter and put it in his pocket as he thought he'd have to phone his father and tell him not to come on Saturday, 'coz he wouldn't want to meet her . . . and him.

While eating the strawberries he looked at Mrs. Everton busying herself around the kitchen and he knew that when they met she wouldn't like his mother, and his mother would certainly dislike her—more than dislike her, hate her in fact, especially when she knew that his dad was a regular visitor here too. It was odd, he thought, that one could stop loving a person, as his mother had done his father, and go off and do her own thing, yet at the same time she didn't want his dad to be happy in any way. People were funny. Grown-up people were very funny, odd. There was no understanding them, or anything they did.

7

Saturday morning started dully; it was raining somewhere over the hills. Sally had pointed that out to him. He had thought it was just a dark cloud but she'd said, "No, it's likely pouring in Hexham, and it'll soon be doing so right down the valley to Newcastle. The clouds are going that way."

He was getting to like Sally. And yet at times he was a bit puzzled when something he would say, which to him might be just a straightforward question, seemed to upset her, and her replies would become drawn out, spasmodic like, as they were the first day he had met her. He couldn't exactly tell why he felt sorry for her but he did. Perhaps it was because Michael always seemed to be going for her. For instance, this morning he'd heard him say, "Stop following Daniel around, and get on with your chores."

He had wanted to say, "I don't mind," but he couldn't, could he?

He had finished sweeping up the storeroom and had gone to the harness room, thinking Michael was there, to ask him if there was anything else he could do before he changed his clothes in preparation for his mother's visit. There was no one in the harness room but there was a door leading out from the end of it into the stable, which was now used as a garage. When he heard Michael's voice coming from there he moved down the room, only to stop at the door as he realized there was a sort of private conversation going on between Michael and his mother. Michael was saying, "Don't worry any more, I'm . . . I'm getting over it. Only one thing I'll ask you and then we'll forget about it. Do . . . do you think I've any relatives at all, alive I mean?"

"Not that I know of, Michael. Your great-grandmother had only one daughter, then she again had only one daughter, who was your mother."

"And . . . and my father?"

"Nothing was known of him except that he had been killed a fortnight before your mother returned home, that was just before you were born. But Michael, as I've said before, from the moment you were born you were mine. I shouldn't say this but I shall: I feel that you are more my son than Sally is my daughter. And what is more, your dad loved you. He used to talk about you with such pride."

"Don't."

Daniel went to turn away, but then he heard his own name mentioned.

"Daniel said that compared to him I should consider myself lucky. I've been thinking about it quite a lot and I'd like you to know now that I do."

"Oh, Michael."

He couldn't see them but it was with a pang of envy that he felt Michael was within his mother's embrace.

He was actually turning stealthily away when Mrs. Everton's voice came to him, saying, "I'm looking forward to seeing this woman, but even before we meet, what I've heard about her doesn't make me think we're going to be bosom friends. How she could walk out on a son like Daniel and, then again, on a husband like Peter I just don't know."

"You like him, don't you?"

"Who? Daniel?"

"No, I don't mean Daniel. You know who I mean, his father. Don't worry, I . . . I wouldn't be mad or anything; life must go on."

"Oh, Michael, don't, don't. I loved your father and it's too soon to think along those lines."

"But the lines are there, aren't they?"

"I don't know. I don't know. Anyway, it's ridiculous. It's likely never entered the man's head."

"From what I've seen of him I wouldn't consider him a fool, so it has entered his head. And there's one thing if nothing else in his favor, and in Daniel's too: they must know something about the upstairs business but they've never let it make any difference. I really think you should tell them."

"No! No! I promised and you promised. Let it stay like that."

"Well, this won't get the work done. Come on."

Daniel could almost see Michael holding out his hand to his mother, and so, on tiptoe, he swiftly made for the door, and then as swiftly crossed the yard to the house.

There was something to hide upstairs after all then. However, what was concerning him more than that was the business about his dad and Mrs. Everton. That would drive his mother mad. Yet why should it? She had her new husband. Still, he knew that if she guessed his dad had taken a fancy to Mrs. Everton she would act up, and then in a way he himself would become more than ever like a shuttlecock between them.

The car was the latest in Jaguars. His mother stepped out of it and onto the narrow wet slimy stones of the farmyard and looked about her.

Mrs. Everton had opened the front door and she was standing just within it as she pushed Daniel forward, saying under her breath, "Go on, boy, meet your mother."

Daniel went down the two steps and across the narrow strip of wet lawn onto the crazy paving path, and there he stopped and looked at his mother coming toward him. She was dressed as he had never seen her before: she looked almost like a fashion model except that she wasn't tall enough to be a model. She was wearing a pale green suit trimmed with gold braid. The skirt had a slit up the side. The heels on her shoes were at least three inches high. Her hair, he noticed immediately, had been done in a different style: it was a mass of tiny corkscrew curls like the way Petula Clark, the singer, wore hers. As he neared her and she put out her hand toward him he noticed that every finger had a ring on it. When she reached up to kiss him he had the desire to push her away. The kissing business had started only after she had remarried.

"My! My! I swear you've put on another six inches. When are you going to stop, boy?" was her greeting.

"Hello there, Danny boy. Or should I say, farmer's boy?" said the man.

"You should say neither."

"Now, now, Daniel. We'll have none of that tone. . . . Where's the woman?"

"Woman?"

"The farmer's wife."

"*Mrs. Everton* is waiting for you in the hall." He turned abruptly about and led the way toward the front door. He heard his mother exclaim as her high heels sank into the wet lawn, "Oh, my goodness! My shoes." And the man exclaim, "Well, I told you we were coming to a farm. You would put them on."

"How do you do? I'm Mrs. Everton, and this is my son Michael . . . and my daughter Sally."

The two women looked at each other and what Mrs. Everton saw was a very smartly dressed woman with a good figure and a pretty face marred by a mouth that drooped at the corners. Her verdict was: a petulant lady.

Daniel's mother looked at the woman before her and saw someone about her own age, perhaps a little older, dressed in a cotton dress that was cheap but that did not mar her well-proportioned figure. This she dubbed to herself as plump. As to the farmer's wife's face, she classed this as ordinary, ignoring the large brown eyes with the natural thick lashes and the creamy skin that required and received no makeup.

"Will you come into the sitting room? Perhaps you would like a cup of tea while you're waiting."

"No, thank you; we must be off soon. George and I have to get back. We are to attend a dinner this evening."

"Oh, that'll be nice." Mrs. Everton smiled from the man to the woman. Then, looking at Daniel, she said,

"That'll be a change for you from roughing it among the cattle."

"Oh, this is a business dinner. The boy isn't ready for that kind of thing yet." The man's lips were pursed while he nodded at Daniel. "Plenty of time for that. Anyway the kids of today, what do they want? Television, records, rock music. Nothing like that in my young days. Work, that's what we had to do, and that's where it's gotten me today, work." He nodded from one to the other and was about to continue when his wife said to Daniel, "Are you ready?"

"No, I'm not ready, Mom."

"What!"

Then all the eyes in the room were on him as he repeated, "I'm not ready, 'coz I'm not coming with you."

"Now, look here, my boy," the man started to say.

"Don't you 'boy' me. And I'm not your boy and never shall be."

"You are coming with us, Daniel, and we'll have no more showing off. You know the situation as well as I do: I have the authority that you shall spend a certain time with me. Now I've let you off for weeks but my patience is at an end. Your father put you up to this, didn't he?"

"He did not. He told me to go with you. But I'm not going back with you, now or ever. I'll soon be sixteen and then you won't be able to do anything about it."

"But until you are sixteen I can do and will do a lot about it." She turned now and looked at Mrs. Everton, saying, "You can help by telling him he must go, that you won't have him here."

"I'm sorry, I can't do that. Peter left him in my care."

"Oh! Oh! It's Peter, is it?"

"Yes." Mrs. Everton now drew herself up to her full height and her voice held a quiet dignity as she said, "And my name is Mary; and my daughter's is Sally and my son's is Michael. You don't stand on ceremony on a farm."

"Look"—the man's voice was quiet now as he appealed to Daniel—"don't cause any more upset, laddie. All right, you'll have it your way in a few months' time, but for the present do as your mother tells you and come along. You won't lose by it. I'll promise you . . . you won't lose by it. I was thinking about getting you a motorbike, that is, later on if you behave yourself. You'll find me very amenable if you behave . . ."

"Shut up! And you can keep your motorbikes. I want nothing from you. As for you, Mom"—he was now looking into his mother's face, which was as tight with anger as when she had failed to get her own way with his father—"as for you," he went on, "all this 'You are my son' business is put on in order to get at me dad, to show him you still have some authority."

"Daniel"—it was Michael's voice speaking now—"go on, get your things and go with your mother. It won't be for long, just a weekend. . . ."

"It won't be just for the weekend," Daniel's mother cried, rounding on Michael; "it'll be for a week or more. He's going to make up for the time he's missed coming. And—" She was now confronting her son again as she cried at him, "And don't think you'll get the better of me today. I'm going to sit here until you are ready to leave." And at this she sat down on a nearby chair.

She now had the attention of everyone in the room, and there was a strange silence for some seconds before Daniel said, "All right, you sit there until I go with you and you'll take root." He stared hard at his mother, then turned around and rushed from the room.

It had been three o'clock when the Jaguar entered the farmyard; it was half-past four when it left, and without Daniel. As Mrs. Everton watched it tearing away down the narrow road she put her hand to her head and, looking at Sally, said, "I've never been so glad to see the back of anybody in my life as that woman. Poor Peter."

"I'd say, poor Daniel."

"Yes"—her mother smiled at her now—"and poor Daniel. As he said, he's been used as a shuttlecock between them for years. Now I wonder where he ran off to?"

"The bottom fields likely."

"Well, go and see if you can find him."

It was a half-hour later when Sally returned. "I can't see him anywhere, Mom," she said. "I went up on the knoll and looked about and I shouted. I went into the copse and through the little wood."

Mrs. Everton looked at the clock and said, "He's been gone over two hours." Going to the back door, she called across the yard, "Michael!" And when Michael appeared at the door of the cow barns, she said, "You don't think Daniel's made for home, hitchhiked it?"

"No, no. He's just keeping out of the way to make sure. Once he's seen the car go he'll be back."

"Had he a coat on?"

"I don't know. He went out of the room, as you know, like a devil in a gale of wind."

"It's looking like rain. I think you should go and have a look for him, because if he's out on the hills and the mist comes down . . . well, you know."

"All right. Give me ten minutes till I finish off, Mom, then I'll go."

"Put your mack on; it's going to turn nasty, I think." She looked up to the sky. Then a minute later, as she fastened the top button of Sally's coat, she said, "Don't go far. We don't want to go out looking for you too."

"That'll be the day when you start looking for me. I know these hills better than you do, Mom, having been with Michael on the trails."

"Go on, Miss Smarty." Her mother pushed her and Sally went off laughing. . . .

Three hours later Mrs. Everton was to remember every word of their light exchanges as she, among others, searched the hills for her daughter and the boy who had come to spend his summer vacation on the farm.

8

As she had said, she knew the hills, but she also knew that no one was safe on the hills in the mist, even the experienced fell walkers. And there it was coming down, floating toward her like a dirty gray cloud.

Sally had come further than she had intended. She was near Poulton's old empty house. Well, it had been an old empty house, but some people had taken it last year and were doing it up on weekends. But the work was progressing slowly and as yet only the roof had been mended. Some of the lower windows had boards across with plastic sheeting stretched over them.

The house stood back about ten yards from a side road that was little more than a track, and from where she stood she couldn't see if there was a car or a van standing to the side of the house. The times she had been this way she had noted that the people often came in a van. She had seen the owner of the van once as he was driving away. He had thick brown hair and a beard. He had lifted his hand in salute to her and she had waved back.

She paused and stared toward the house. Could Daniel have taken shelter in there? He had likely run out without a coat, and the mist was already penetrating her own mack and making her shiver. Yet she doubted whether he would go into a strange house even if it were empty, unless of course he was asked in.

She paused for a moment, deliberating whether to hurry on back home or to go and see if she could look in one of the windows. He might even be sheltering in the outhouses at the back; there was a kind of courtyard there. The last time she had seen it, it had been strewn with grass, but she had imagined it could be nice if it were cleared.

The decision as to what to do seemed to have been made by her legs, because now she was running toward the house. The double wooden farm-type gate was wide open. She stepped off the rough path and hurried through the tall wet grass to the front window on the left side of the door. There had been fresh plastic sheeting put over the boards here, and she could see nothing inside. She passed the front door and attempted to look through the other window, but this too was covered in the same way.

She hurried around the side of the house, her footsteps muted by the matted grass. There was no vehicle in the courtyard but she noticed immediately that the back door was slightly ajar. She went to it and pushed it open, then stood transfixed at what she saw, as did the three occupants of the room—the two men who were standing and the bound figure on the floor.

When the man with the beard sprang toward her there

came into her head that recognizable whirling that made her mouth spring wide and dragged up from the depths of her a great protesting scream.

The man had grabbed her by the shoulders, but now he almost threw her from him and, her eyeballs rolling, she fell to the floor in a screaming, writhing bundle of twitching limbs.

When at last the terrifying sound faded, three pairs of eyes watched her teeth digging into her lower lip as her body became almost rigid; then, as if from a balloon, the air seemed to be let out of her and her limbs relaxed and she lay supine. The only sound now was her breathing, which was like a series of snorts.

"Good God! That was a fit. . . . She had a fit!"

"Aye." Billy Combo looked down on Sally as he remarked, "She's given to them. That's another thing they tried to hide. But this is a nice kettle of fish, two of 'em."

"What are we gonna do?"

"I'll have to think." Combo rubbed his chin with his hand. Then, glancing at the bound and gagged figure of Daniel, he said, "I know what I'm gonna do with that 'un. Right from the start I knew what I was gonna do with him. If only the damned truck hadn't broken down."

"I told you we should have made another contact."

"Don't talk crazy, Arthur. Go to one of the garages, should we, and say, 'Lend us a van, mister, to transport stolen sheep down to Shields quay'? Aw, man! I think most of your brains is in your beard, and you'll be a dead loss if ever you shave that off. Look, I'll go down to the main road and phone. And you get in the shed there and skin 'em ready. And see you put plenty of potatoes on top of each one in plastic bags. We don't want any slip up on the dock side; it nearly happened last time."

"Why don't you just let them go to the butchers? There's plenty'll take them."

"And for what? Pin money, compared with what the foreigners give us for a few extra miles of cartage. Have sense, man. Now go on, get out and get started."

"What about her? She wants tying up an' all, doesn't she?"

"If past times is anything to go by she'll sleep till the morning."

"Look, I don't like it. I can understand about him"—the man nodded toward Daniel—"but she . . . she's only a bit of a lass."

"Don't worry. We'll drop her off somewhere along the way, miles out, and when they find her we'll be well in the middle of the ocean. And this lanky townie with us." He had turned swiftly and jabbed Daniel in the side with his boot. As Daniel's eyes blazed back at him Combo bent over him and said, "Aye, you can look like that, but before I say farewell to you, me lad, you won't be able to see out of either of them. You'll regret the day you showed me up."

Helplessly, Daniel watched the two men go out of the room, closing the door behind them. And from where he sat propped against the wall he looked at the limp form of Sally and, for the moment forgetting his own fate, he was overwhelmed by a feeling of sadness and pity. The mystery of the screaming was solved; but oh, how he wished for her sake it could have had some other solution. Poor, poor Sally. That's why her mother wouldn't let her go to dances; that's why she couldn't ride. He recalled now the conversation at the bottom of the stairs between the brother and sister and he knew that she had been pleading with Michael not to mention the fact that she was epileptic. That was why, too, she slept up in the attic when there were strangers in the house. Yet didn't they know that her screams could be heard down below? Well, his father hadn't heard them and he himself had only heard them because he was a light sleeper.

Oh, if she'd only wake up. If he could only get this gag out of his mouth. He could hardly breathe. And his arms were breaking; the rope was cutting into his wrists.

In a sudden desperate movement he fell onto his side and wriggled his body toward Sally until his feet were touching her shoulder, and in no gentle fashion he now began to push her.

For almost five minutes he pushed at her, thrusting his feet against her arm. But in spite of all his efforts her body remained inert, her head lying to the side, the saliva running out of the corner of her mouth. . . .

Always after a seizure Sally had been made comfortable. Usually a water bottle was put at her feet, blankets were tucked around her, the thin bone ruler that had been placed between her teeth to prevent her biting her lips was drawn away, and her hair was stroked gently from her forehead. All this had helped her toward relaxed sleep. Never before had she been pushed, even thumped, into wakefulness. She was aware of a great dizziness in her head. She felt very tired. She wanted to sleep, but something was stopping her. Somewhere in her mind a voice was crying, "Mom! Mom!"

The voice grew louder and she now felt herself being rocked from side to side. The voice in her head changed and now called, "Michael! Michael!" The rocking was still going on. She was floating upward through a blackness that slowly turned to gray. The rocking was hurting her; her arm ached. The gray light became white; it was on her eyelids. She wished Michael would stop rocking her; he was hurting her arm. Why was he doing it? He had never hurt her on purpose. He sometimes got angry with her when she acted silly and got into a temper about having fits. Why should she have fits? Other girls didn't have fits. She couldn't have any fun, not like other girls. Oh dear. Oh dear. Her head was going around. If only he would stop hurting her arm . . . *Oh, that was an awful push! Why was he doing it?*

Slowly she opened her eyes. Her lids felt heavy. She looked upward. The rocking had stopped. Where was she? The ceiling was dirty. This wasn't her bedroom. Slowly she turned her head to the side, and as if the mist had invaded the room she saw through it the trussed figure of Daniel. His head was on a level with hers, only some distance away. There was a rag hanging from his mouth. She should pull it out, but she was so tired.

As she went to close her eyes again the rocking started once more and she blinked, rapidly now. It wasn't Michael, it was Daniel, and he was kicking her, kicking her arm. He wanted something. Now he was wriggling toward her. His face was near her; she only had to put her hand up and pull that rag from his mouth. She stared into his face. His head was moving in a pitying sort of way. She wanted to help him, but she was tired; all she wanted to do was sleep. He was moving his head down now by the side of her arm. His cheek was near her hand. Go on, she said to herself, do that for Daniel, because you like him. He's been nicer to you than any of the Threadgill boys. They had never wanted to walk with her or talk with her. . . .

There, she had made the effort and she was looking into Daniel's face again. His mouth was working and he was spitting. It wasn't nice to spit, but likely the rag was dirty.

"Sally! Sally! Wake up! Wake up! Do you hear?"

"What?"

"Come on, wake up! Sally! Listen. You can hear me, can't you? You can understand what I'm saying? Look at me, Sally. Sally! My life depends upon you, upon your getting home and telling Michael and Mr. Threadgill and the others. Oh, Sally! Sally, wake up. Come on, wake up!"

"Oh, Daniel." Sally had pulled herself onto her elbow now and, looking at him, she said, "I . . . I feel dizzy."

"Kneel up. Come on. Come on."

Slowly she did as he bade her. Then, looking at his ankles, she said, "I . . . I can't untie them. I'm very tired, Daniel."

"I know you can't untie them. You couldn't in any case—it's tarred rope and they've made a good job of it. But look. Go on outside. Go quietly, and get home."

"I . . . I can't, Daniel. I'm . . . I'm very tired."

"Sally!" He had his face close to hers now. "Listen to me. Do you want me to die?"

"Oh no, Daniel. No, Daniel."

"Well then, get on your feet and get home. And listen. Listen carefully. They're taking the sheep, and me, to a boat that's lying berthed in Shields. Have you got that? A boat that's lying berthed in Shields. It'll be sailing on the morning tide. Listen. Listen, Sally. Tell them it's a foreign boat. . . . Oh good, good, you're standing up. Now go on, quietly."

"I'll . . . I'll fall."

"No, you won't. Once you get in the air, you'll be better. Oh, Sally, go on, quickly."

As if still in a dream, Sally stumbled toward the door. When she pulled it open and it creaked loudly, Daniel closed his eyes tightly and bowed his head, expecting any minute that the big bearded fellow would come dashing toward her and thrust her into the room again. But there was no sound from outside. For a moment he thought she must have fallen down and was lying there inert again. But then his attention was brought around to the sound of footsteps beyond the window. They were light, as if someone were walking in slippered feet on a carpet. Again he closed his eyes. She had gotten that far. And feeling so far relieved, he edged himself back toward the wall and forced himself up into the position in which they had left him. But now as he waited for Combo's return he was filled with fear such as he had never experienced before.

Outside, the mist was thick and Sally stumbled into it, not really conscious of the direction she was taking. Twice she tripped and fell down. The second time she had a great desire to stay where she was, lying on the wet hillside, but her shivering brought her to her feet again.

The mist was coming in patches. One minute she could see yards ahead, the next she was enveloped as if in swathes of gauze. In one clear patch she saw the road ahead and a van passing along it. The sight of the van stirred something within her that told her she must get home quickly. Yes, she must get home. But which way was home?

She was still so tired, so very sleepy. At one point she found she was crying. She hadn't known she was crying; she had thought it was the mist running down her face, until she began to whimper, "Oh, Mom. Mom." Then she was adding another name: "Michael. Michael. Michael." And soon she was calling another name and out loud now: "Daniel. Daniel."

When she stumbled against a small stone wall, she smiled to herself. She knew where she was now. It was Mr. Beaconsfield's lambing shed. Oh, that was nice. Likely there was straw inside there and she could lie down and go to sleep again and be warm. Oh, she wanted to be warm and to sleep.

She crawled into the small stone hut and lay down on the damp straw, and within minutes she had fallen asleep again.

"Dear God! What could have happened to them?" Mary Everton looked from Farmer Threadgill to his companion, Farmer Newberry, then on to Peter Jones, and when she said, "Not a sign of either of them?" it was a question, and it was Farmer Threadgill who answered, "No, Mary, and it's as black as ink out there. It's hopeless looking further until the morning."

"What!" Daniel's father rounded on them. "We've got lanterns, haven't we? And if the rescue team can go out, we can . . . at least, I can."

"Excuse me for saying so, but you know nothing about these parts, or its weather, Mr. Jones. The search party will have given up by now and we should be hearing from them at any minute. As for the children, they've likely found some shelter, in an old barn or underneath a knoll of some sort. There's the phone now. That'll likely be Jim Wade."

Mary Everton ran down the kitchen toward the hall doorway, there to see Michael picking up the phone.

Then she watched his mouth widen and his face brighten and she heard him say, "Oh, thank you, Mr. Beaconsfield! Thank you. We'll be over immediately."

He banged the phone down and, turning to his mother, he said, "They've found her . . . Mr. Beaconsfield. She was fast asleep in the lambing hut."

They exchanged a quick glance that spoke as plainly as words, saying: she must have had one of her turns.

They were both in the kitchen now crying their news, and amid the bustle of getting into coats, Mr. Jones's voice came quietly: "And Daniel . . . is he with her?"

Mary Everton now looked sadly at him, saying, "He . . . he didn't say," she said; "he . . . he only mentioned her name. But . . . but likely he's found shelter too. He's certain to. Don't worry." She put her hand out and touched his sleeve, then said softly, "Go with Michael to pick her up. I'll stay here in case there's further news."

Mr. Jones said nothing to this but turned silently away and followed Michael and the farmers out of the kitchen. And Mary, once the door was closed, began to busy herself, filling hot water bottles, putting extra blankets on Sally's bed, setting a pan of broth on the stove to heat; and when all this was done she sat to the side of the fire, her eyes on the door, her ears alert for the return of the Land-Rover.

She hadn't long to wait.

Michael laid Sally down on the rug before the fire, saying as he did so, "She's frozen stiff. Another couple of hours out there and she'd have been a goner. Get something hot into her, Mom."

The warmth, the tender hands, the hot liquid that was

sliding effortlessly down her gullet brought Sally some way back to consciousness. When she opened her eyes and saw her mother's face above her, she had the feeling she had been sent with some message and that she should now deliver it. But what had she been sent for? What had she to bring back?

"There, there, my dear. You're all right." The voice was soothing, sleep-inducing again. But she struggled against it. She had been sent on an errand of some sort and she must tell her mother. But what had she to tell her?

As she felt a warm wet cloth passing over her mouth she remembered the errand, at least part of it. It was to do with the cloth in Daniel's mouth. She opened her eyes and said, "Daniel."

"Yes, dear? Yes . . . Daniel? Where is he? Did you see him?"

"Gag, Mom."

"What did she say?"

Michael, who was kneeling on the mat at Sally's side, turned his head and, looking up at Mr. Jones, he said, "It sounded like gag."

"And to me too." Mr. Jones bent forward and appealed to Mary: "Can't you wake her up? She might be able to tell us something."

"I doubt it at this stage." Mary turned her face toward him. "She must have had a turn."

"A turn?"

"Yes; she is given to epileptic fits."

Mr. Jones felt his face stretch slightly. So that was it: the screaming, the goings-on in the night. Why on earth had they kept it a secret? And he said as much. "Why have you tried to hide it, I mean, her being epileptic?"

"Because she was so ashamed of anybody knowing. She can go months on end and not have one, then excitement, something new like your visit and being in the company . . . sympathetic company of Daniel, set her off again the first night you were here.

"She sleeps up in the attic when there're guests. But we rarely have guests, except one or two members of the family who know of her condition. Even then she sleeps in the far room in the attic in case she should disturb anyone. You didn't hear her?"

"I didn't the first night, but Daniel did."

"I told you." Michael was nodding at his mother now. "He looked at me as if I'd been hammering her. Stupid, anyway, to try and keep the thing hidden; it always comes out sooner or later. She's got to face it, I've told her."

"She's only a child yet, Michael; she doesn't really understand. Anyway, there is hope." Mary now looked up at Mr. Jones. "I understand there's been a breakthrough and that there's a new treatment. It doesn't answer for everybody and as yet only for light petit mal cases and these have been cured. But unfortunately Sally's isn't a light case. Still, the attacks are not nearly so frequent as they used to be. She's on special pills and up till now they've worked wonders."

"How long will it be before she comes round?" The question from Mr. Jones sounded urgent and Mary answered, "Oh, she can sleep for eight solid hours, sometimes less. She must already have been sleeping for sometime now."

"You couldn't waken her? Her mentioning Daniel, she might . . ."

"It was likely only because she was looking for him,"

Michael said quietly now. "If she had seen him he would have been with her, wouldn't he?"

"Yes, yes, I suppose so." Mr. Jones straightened his back and turned away, muttering as he did so, "Damn that woman! Why couldn't she leave him alone?"

9

Daniel thought that Combo was about to go completely insane when he came back into the room and found Sally gone. There was another man with him, short, thickset with ginger hair, and Combo turned to him and screamed, "She's gone! Where the . . . !" There followed a string of expletives as he rushed to the door, from where he shouted, "You, Arthur!" then immediately turned back and, approaching Daniel, began to scream at the top of his voice. His arms flailing, his feet stamping, he looked as if he was dancing with rage. When finally his hands went around Daniel's throat and he screamed at him, "Where is she?" Daniel, almost choking, gasped, "Home. Home." Combo let go of his throat and turned to where the bearded man was now standing in the doorway, and he screamed at him, "Where the hell do you think you've been? What have you been doing? The girl's gone!"

"Gone?" The man stepped further into the room and stood looking down at Daniel. "Where's she gone?" he said stupidly. "What've you done with her?"

As Combo yelled at him, "Don't be such a senseless idiot!" Daniel yelled as loudly, "I sent her home. By now she'll be there and you can all look out. As for you, Combo, it won't be just a black eye you'll get. When Michael and those farmers get you . . . get all of you, you won't be able to walk to jail. I'll tell you that, the lot of you. . . ."

The kick that Daniel received from Combo's boot knocked him onto his side and almost made him vomit. He lay gasping with the pain, and for a second was only conscious of a confusion of angry voices without making any coherent sense of them before Combo, forcing Daniel's mouth open by the simple method of digging his fingers and thumb into his cheeks, stuffed the dirty rag back into it again, while hissing, "You'll be sorry you ever crossed me, lad. Just you wait and see."

"I'm gettin' out of this," the short man said; "I didn't like it in the first place."

"You're in it as much as we are and you'll stay and see it through now."

"You should have sold them to the butchers as I said." It was the bearded man, Arthur, speaking and as Combo hoisted Daniel roughly to his feet he cried at his mate, "Don't talk through the top of your hat! Sell them for what? Pin money, when we can get twenty pounds a head from the captain? Shut up and start loading."

"What about the skins?"

"Leave them. If that little fit case has reached home the skins won't be any surprise to them when they arrive here. . . . Come on, you, jump!"

Daniel tried to hop but he fell forward onto his knees, and Combo called toward the small man who had already gone into the yard, "Give me a hand with this one, Tollgood. He's not skinned yet but he soon will be."

The man Tollgood came back into the room and said to Combo, "What do you intend to do with him?"

"You leave that to me."

"I don't want to be in on any dirty business."

"Who's askin' you? Just drive us to the quay."

"You'll never get him on board without being seen. There's the river police and always somebody about."

"In fog like this? The radio says it's all over the place. Anyway, he won't be walkin', hoppin', or jumpin' on board; he'll be in a sack like the rest."

"I don't like it. Sheep's one thing, people another."

"Look, get a hold of his arm and get him into the back of the van, because, let me tell you, if you don't get at that wheel pretty soon it'll be like he said—we ourselves mightn't be able to walk to jail."

Between them they now dragged and hopped Daniel to the back of the van, and there Combo, standing him up against an opened door, reached inside the van and pulled out two sacks. Then suddenly he pushed Daniel so that he fell backward onto the van floor with his legs dangling downward, and ignoring the excruciating moan that penetrated the gag, he pulled a sack over Daniel's legs and tied it around the boy's waist. The second sack he pulled over Daniel's head but left loose. Now he commanded, "Heave him!"

As Daniel felt himself being thrust among the bodies of the sheep, he thought for a moment he was going to suffocate. He was so full of fear that, had he been able, he felt sure he would have screamed like a girl.

As the minutes passed and he felt more carcasses thrust around him, he prayed earnestly that Sally would have reached home and that the men would be on their way. But when the van began to move down the uneven road, a sense of utter hopelessness enveloped him.

He had no idea how long the journey took, he only knew that every minute his fear increased, if that was possible, and that he had to fight to keep breathing. He knew too that all the hate Combo was capable of had been concentrated against himself. And what would this hate cause him to do? Daniel shuddered at the thought that entered his head. If they got him on board a ship he could easily be dumped. He had heard stories of it happening before, especially after a body had come in on the tide.

The thought made him struggle, but his struggling only settled the carcasses of the sheep more firmly around him. . . . He was going to suffocate. He wanted air. If only he could get this rag out of his mouth. . . . If only he could get his head out of the sack. If only . . . if only.

If only he had gone with his mother when she'd asked him, or, more to the point, if only she hadn't come pestering him, this would never have happened.

He mustn't give way, he must try to keep a clear head. Surely somebody somewhere would come to his aid. That other man, the driver.

Don't be silly. Don't be silly. His body slumped. He stopped struggling, both mentally and physically, and lay limp awaiting events.

He was only half-conscious when he felt the sack being lifted from his head. When the light flashed into his eyes, he screwed them up against it. But he could not close his ears to Combo's voice, hissing softly at him now, "Feel that," whereupon he experienced a sharp jab in his neck that would have made him cry out in pain if that had been possible. Combo went on, "In a few ticks you'll be slung over somebody's shoulder and feel yourself being carried. Now you make one wriggle in protest and this will go right through your gullet." Again he felt the pressure of the knife against his neck, but not so hard this time.

The next instant the sack was pulled over his head again and he lay still, listening. They were removing the sheep and doing it very quietly.

When his legs were tugged forward and pulled over the edge of the van he thought his back would break, and he groaned inwardly, only for this to be checked when he felt his body being hauled upward. And then he knew he was being hoisted over someone's shoulder. Whoever was carrying him, he realized, must be very strong, for he himself was no lightweight. And under his weight the person's steps were even, until his gait changed and then Daniel knew they were ascending a slope . . . a gangway. Yes, that was it—he was being taken on board the boat.

The steps were on the level once more; then when he felt he was going to fall headfirst downward, he knew they were descending a ladder set at a steep angle.

Again he was being borne along on the level; then once more his head was thrust forward and within seconds he was dropped to the ground. The next minute the sack was taken from his head and he was immediately aware of two things: first, he was staring up at a man who seemed to be of enormous proportions; and second, that the air he was breathing now stank with a rankness that was sickening.

"Not very light sheep, that one." The man was obviously a foreigner and he was speaking to someone who was descending an iron ladder. It was Combo, and Combo answered the big man, saying, "What did you take the sack off him for?"

"Can't cause no harm now. And I wanted to see what he looked like. . . . Just a boy—big, but still a boy. Why?"

Combo answered the big man's question by repeating his word: "Why? He knows why and I know why."

"Captain will want straighter answer than that. Captain won't like it."

"He'll like it all right, because if that one was to go free" —he aimed his foot toward Daniel but didn't reach him— "I wouldn't be the only one on thin ice for the next year or so. He knows too much, a damn sight too much."

"He has no passport. What'll he do at other side?"

Combo turned away toward the ladder, saying, "Where he's going he won't need a passport, Blondie."

Now the big man turned his gaze from Combo and looked down on Daniel, and his eyes narrowed slightly before he said, "No?"

And Combo repeated, "No."

"Oh." The big man continued to stare at Daniel for a moment or so longer; then, shaking his head slowly, he lifted one shoulder upward before turning away and following Combo up the ladder.

When the iron hatch clanged shut, Daniel was left in a blackness that was frightening. He seemed to feel it on his skin. His heart began to beat rapidly. He seemed more afraid now of this utter darkness than he was of his impending end. And then there was the silence. But he needn't have worried about this for his legs jerked upward as something ran across them . . . a rat. He was in the bowels of a ship and there were always rats in ships, so he understood.

If only he could get this filthy rag out of his mouth. Combo had secured it with a piece of string that ran in between his teeth and was knotted at the back of his head.

If only he could get his hands free.

If only, if only. . . . If only he could stop himself saying that. He ceased his struggling and lay limp on the filthy floor, and there settled on him an overwhelming feeling of despair. He knew now it was very unlikely that when Sally did reach home she'd remember anything about a ship. Even if she did, there were so many ships coming and going up the river. And even if they started searching now, there was little hope that they would reach this one before it sailed.

How long he had lain in the blackness he didn't know. He did know that for a time he must either have fallen asleep or become unconscious, which was a good thing because his body was now so racked with pain that it was almost unbearable. But when he heard the hatch being lifted once more, he made an effort to raise himself on his elbow and to peer upward. And he felt a strange stirring of curiosity when he realized that whoever was coming down into the hole was doing so very stealthily.

But his curiosity was obliterated by a feeling of panic as he thought: It's Combo. He's going to do me in now.

Painful as the action was, he pulled himself into a sitting position. When the light from a flashlight almost blinded him he turned his head away, then jerked it back again as a thick North-country voice said, "It's all right, it's only me. Eeh! My lad, you're in a state. Got you trussed up like a chicken. Here, let's get rid of that."

The next minute Daniel drew in one great long gasp of

breath and although the air was foul, the first gulp of it going down his throat tasted sweet.

As he sat gasping he looked at the figure bending over him and illuminated now in the light, a thin sharp face above a thin short body. At first Daniel thought he was looking at a young boy, yet there was an adultness about both the face and the voice that belied this. For now he was speaking, saying, "I'm Jackie Cummings. I'm a hand on this old tank, an' as a rule I usually mind me own business. That's how you keep out of the water." He grinned now, and then went on, "An' you can take me word for it there's some business goes on here that would raise your Aunt Mabel's eyebrows. But this last . . . I mean you—" His voice now sank to a whisper as he asked, "How did you get on the wrong side of that little rat, the Combo fellow?"

"I came on him stealing sheep."

"An' he's gonna do you in for that?"

There was a pause before Daniel said, "It seems like it."

"It doesn't *seem* like it, it's a sure thing. He means to finish you off. This is the third trip I've come across him. I didn't like him on first sight an' I like him less now. And Blondie isn't for it either."

"Blondie?"

"Aye, he's the mate. He brought you down here. He's not above using a knife himself where it's necessary—I've seen him at it—but he doesn't like this last affair. I heard him try to talk the little fellow out of it. But no, you're to be thrown off the deep end. They're gonna keep you until tomorrow night. That's if everything goes according to plan. But the last word's the captain's, an' if I know anything about him he won't like this set-up one bit. Not that he's afraid of dumpin' anybody. Oh no. Shave his mother's hair off and sell it, he would; skin a louse for its hide, that's our dear captain. And the little rat Combo doesn't know him like the rest of us does. For you know somethin'?"

Daniel remained quiet, just waiting, and the young fellow went on, "They're already takin' bets on what the captain will do with Combo after the little fellow's finished with you. Likely see he follows you down an' so quick too that he'll keep you company. That's if you go down." There followed a short silence before Daniel's companion ended, "Well, what are we gonna do about you?"

And Daniel replied quickly, "You could loosen these ropes and let me make a fight for it."

"Aye, aye, that's what I thought of doin' in the first place. I didn't risk me neck comin' down here just to say hello. Yet even if they found me, Blondie himself wouldn't dare do anything to me. I'm in with the captain, you see. I make him laugh an' I listen to his prattle when he's drunk. He cries sometimes, aye, he does, a great big fellow like him. He had two sons and he lost them. That's why he's taken to me. But he's gonna get a surprise one of these days for he's gonna lose me too."

All the time the young man was talking he was pulling at the tarred ropes, then impatiently he let rip an oath, ending, "Never undo these! Where's me knife?"

Within seconds Daniel's arms slowly fell apart and he groaned audibly. Next, when his ankles were freed he turned over, and on his hands and knees crawled a short distance before levering himself to his feet with the aid of a stanchion.

When at last he was upright, he turned and leaned his

back for support against the strength of the stanchion; then, looking down on his rescuer, he said, "Thank you. Even if I get no further than this, thank you."

"I've been thinkin'."

"Yes?"

"It's not likely anybody will come near you until the captain comes aboard. That should be an hour afore high tide around seven o'clock. Now at six they change the watch. It wouldn't be any use makin' a run for it at night unless you're a very good swimmer. Are you?"

"No."

"Anyway, on the quayside the gangway's up. And there's always a lookout there, either big Nick or Andy the Norwegian. But Nick's worse than any Norwegian—he's mean, is Nick, another Combo type only twice the size. No, the best time is when they change the watch. There's no ceremony about that—a couple go down and a couple come up. That'll be your chance during the time nobody's on deck. You say you're no swimmer; how are you at jumpin'?"

"What do you mean?"

"Well, she'll be ridin' a bit high about that time. You might have to take a runnin' jump from the deck onto the quay."

"I can jump. But what'll happen if they find out you've helped me escape?"

"Oh, I wouldn't have helped you escape, not me. There's one or two fellows on this ship who are known to do anythin' for a bribe. The captain'll get it out of them. They'll confess to anythin' if it'll save their necks. And it won't in the long run." He grinned. Daniel shook his head in wonderment at such cool courage, and his thoughts went back again to his early schooldays and young

Tommy Thirkell. It would seem that what little men lost in stature they gained in gumption. "How did you come to join this ship?" he asked.

"Oh, that's a long story, but cut short it's simple. I was on the run, the police was after me, and it was reform school if I was caught. Now, as I understand it, in reform school you have to do what you're told and it was that very thing that caused me to play the nick so often. And then again not havin' any settled home to speak of . . . well, I passed through four homes in five years."

"Your parents?"

"Oh, me dad was killed on the railway when I was five, me mother died a year after, and me granny was too old to take me, or too damned lazy. Old, did I say? She was a young kind of granny, frivolous as they come. Believe it or not her main aim in life was dancin'." He chuckled low in his throat now. "Anyway I was sleepin' rough an' one night I came along the quay here in the dark. There was somethin' goin 'on, unloadin' on the quiet, an' where angels fear to tread, as the sayin' goes, I stepped in an' gave them a hand. The fellows took me aboard. Took me, did I say? They nearly kicked me backside in behind an' me face in front. I was nearly in the same predicament as you are, only not quite, for the captain laughed himself silly when he knew I was runnin' from the police. Right from the beginning I talked back to him, cheeked him. He seemed to take a fancy to me after that. How old was I, he asked. 'On eighteen,' I said. . . . 'Well, what's two years one way or the other?' So I was in. And I enjoyed it at first, sort of felt I'd fallen on me feet, but that feeling's worn off. I've been thinkin' about doing the skip many a time, only where would I skip to?" His face took on a solemn look. "This is the only home I know of. And they're all right to me, no matter what they are to other folks. So I suppose it's a life on the ocean wave, and as long as I keep me mouth shut, me eyes closed, an' me ears bunged up, I'll survive."

"How old are you really?"

"Well, the answer me granny would have given you to that would have been, as old as me tongue and a little older than me teeth; but for your secret information I'm eighteen come next Wednesday, but twenty on the books here."

Daniel shook his head in mute admiration and not a little envy for his newfound liberator, and when the young fellow now asked, "I suppose you're hungry?" he answered, "No, no, I'm not. But I'm dry, thirsty. My throat's parched with that rag."

"Aye, well, I should have thought of that. . . . It annoys me when I don't think of everythin'." He made a sound like a small deprecating laugh, then said softly, "I'll be back. I can't say when, but I'll bring you a drink and some grub. Look." He handed the flashlight to Daniel now, saying, "Hang on to that. But listen, as soon as you hear the slightest thing up above, even if you think it's me, put the light out and get down on the floor and put those ropes around your ankles again and your hands behind you. If it's any of the crew I don't suppose they'll come right down; they'll just want to see that you're alive. Here." He bent down swiftly and picked up the rag. "Don't lose that. Stick it in your mouth, help make up the picture. Well, I'm away."

As the young fellow turned toward the ladder Daniel said, "Thank you. Thank you, Jack."

The sharp face came around on the shoulder and on a grin said, "Jackie. Jack's too old."

"Jackie."

As Daniel watched the slight figure ascend the ladder like a monkey climbing a tree he found himself praying: "Dear Lord, let his plan succeed. Oh please, let his plan succeed."

His father always said that people would promise God all kinds of things if only he would answer their requests, and in this moment he wanted to add, "I'll do anything in the future if you get me out of this: go and see me mother, work hard, never get into trouble." But he checked himself. That kind of plea sounded too much like being a lie, because he knew that if he did get out of here, he'd still dislike going to see his mother, for it was she who had brought him to this. And as for never getting into trouble, well, what was he going to do with his life—go into a monastery? Why was he thinking like this, silly like? His mind was in a turmoil.

He now flashed the light around him. The place seemed full of old rope, boxes, and an assortment of what looked like odd wheels and broken ironwork. It came to him that if anyone but Jackie should come down here he could take an iron bar to them. But what good would that do? He couldn't hope to knock out all the crew. No, he must do as Jackie said, pretend he was still tied up and wait for the dawn.

It was almost two hours later when Jackie again descended the ladder. Drawing from underneath his coat a flat bottle like a whiskey flask, he said, "It's cold tea but it'll quench your thirst. And there's some meat sandwiches. It's all I could scrounge from me supper."

While Daniel gulped at the cold tea, which tasted bitter

yet was so refreshing, Jackie dropped onto his haunches in front of him, quietly saying, "There's a lot of talk goin' on upstairs about you. Some of them don't want that Combo sailing with us. But apparently he's blotted his copy book, so much that the police'll be after him. . . . Who's the little lass who has fits?"

"She's . . . she's the farmer's daughter. Her father died recently; her mother runs the farm." He now related to Jackie the whole story of what had happened with Combo on the farm, and he finished by saying, "Combo knows his number is up because once the police get him he'll do a tidy stretch of time, for the sheep stealing has been going on for a long time."

"Yes, yes, it has." Jackie now scratched the back of his neck. "They rear some very good sheep in Northumberland; we've had them on a good many trips, though it's only on the last three we've seen the bold boy Combo at the head of affairs. Anyway, he's determined to sail with us, not only to see you get your deserts but so that he can make, as he says, a fresh start someplace else. I suggested Australia, 'coz as I pointed out there's many more sheep there, but I think they hang them—I mean the sheep stealers—when they find them. All the others laughed, but he didn't. It wouldn't be long, I should think, afore he has the same feelin' for me as he has for you. I'll have to watch out if he does more than this one trip. But still, as I said, he too may be going down to Davy Jones's locker. You know, he made a funny quip about that when talking about you. Jones, he said they called you, D. Jones."

Daniel lowered his head and bit on his lip. It was odd about Davy Jones's locker. It would be very strange, wouldn't it, if he were to end up in the sea, because every now and again it seemed to dawn on someone to tease him about his name. It happened often at school when a teacher would call out, "D. Jones!" In fact, when he was in the old school they gave him the nickname of Locker. Locker Jones, they would call him. . . .

"You're not eatin' those sandwiches."

"I will shortly. I'm so grateful for the drink."

"You've got decent parents?"

Daniel hesitated for a moment before answering: "Yes; yes, you could say that, but they're separated."

"Separated?"

"Yes. My mother's married again. But, I suppose you could call her a decent parent, a bit too decent if overcaring is to be counted, at least since she's remarried. But my dad's all right. He and I get along fine."

"Who do you live with?"

"With me dad. But I have to see my mother every month. That's why I'm here now." He thumbed toward the floor.

"Say that again."

"That's why I'm here now. You see, she came to the farm where I was on vacation and demanded I go back with her to Carlisle, work out my time, so to speak. And I walked out, ran out, across the fields and straight into Combo and his activities. But I suppose you could still say they're decent parents."

"She's your mother." Jackie's voice was grim now. "Why on earth didn't you want to go and stay with her?"

Daniel didn't answer for a moment. There had been a condemning note in his new friend's voice and under other circumstances he would have likely retorted, "Mind your own business." But now he answered quietly, "It's hard to explain. She . . . she didn't seem to bother with me before she walked out on Dad, and even during the two years she was away before the divorce went through she made no demands on me, but once she had married this man–he . . . he's got money you see–she seemed bent on showing me how well she'd done for herself."

"Hadn't your dad a job?"

"Yes, he's a gardener. But that wasn't ambitious enough for Mom."

"Eeh . . . folks!" Jackie turned away, his shaking head expressing his condemnation. "Folks is funny." Then, bringing his gaze back to Daniel, he muttered, "I'd have given me eye teeth for a mom and dad. I can only remember me mom vaguely, but I know she was nice. And I've a picture of me dad runnin' round a room with me on his shoulders. But after they went everybody changed. Yet I may be wrong; perhaps it was just me that changed and everybody else remained the same. Anyway, as I see it now"–a twinkle came into his eyes–"you'd have been better off, lad, if you'd gone with your mother. Wouldn't you?"

"Yes, yes, you're right. And it isn't the first time I've said that within the last few hours."

"Well now, I must be off and about me lawful duties, which is to get into me bunk. But by the way, if I was you I'd sleep with one eye open, so you can get back into your tied-up pose afore anybody gets down that ladder, 'coz you never know. Although I don't think you'll have any visitors. And by the way, if I don't see you afore the mornin', do a little limbering up now and again to get your joints oiled, because you might have to do some sprintin' even afore you land on the quay. Be seein' you."

"Yes, be seeing you, Jackie."

Once the hatch was closed, Daniel again arranged the cut ropes near his ankles to the side of the stanchion against which he was leaning. The rag he put in the breast pocket of his coat, ready to whip out. Then he settled down, determined to keep awake during the long hours ahead of him. One thing he didn't do was to turn off the light; he'd have to take a chance on the battery running out, but as long as the light was on, the rats would keep their distance. At least he hoped so.

10

Daniel was finding that even fear could not keep sleep at bay, for every now and again his head would droop forward; and then he would jerk it up, blink his eyes rapidly, stretch his mouth, and peer around into the shadowy dimness.

He was doing so again and, realizing that the flashlight battery was running out, he was calculating that it must be an hour or so since Jackie had left him, or that it might even be the middle of the night, for he had no idea of the time. Then a movement above the hatch brought him alert. Bending swiftly, he put the ropes into place around his ankles, stuffed the filthy gag back into his mouth, pushed his hands behind him, then twisted the rope around them. But just as the hatch opened he realized he hadn't switched off the light. Thrusting his hand out, he grabbed it and the next minute he was in blackness, listening to the recognized voices of Combo and the Swede. And it was the Swede who was saying, "Time enough. Time enough. Stay where you are. You're a greedy little man, aren't you? In all ways. Greedy for revenge, greedy for money. Anyway, once the captain's aboard he'll decide what's to be done."

Now came Combo's voice, hissing, "I know what's to be done, and it's going to be done, captain or no captain."

"Ho, ho! Big mouth and little body. You talk like that to captain. Yes, you do that."

There was a laugh now. Then a strong light flashed down into Daniel's eyes, but it was directed upward as the mate descended the ladder.

When again the flashlight shone into Daniel's face, the mate said, "Well, how goes it?"

Daniel could only continue to blink into the light, and the mate said, "Uncomfortable? Yes, you would be."

Suddenly he bent his tall thick body downward, his eyes focused on an object partly tucked under Daniel's side. Then he slowly put out his hand and gently lifted up the flashlight.

Straightening his back, he stood staring down on it where it lay in his outstretched palm, speaking rapidly and softly, apparently in his own tongue, as he did so. Then, his eyes narrowing, he looked down toward Daniel's ankles and he slowly laid the small light down again on the boards. His hand now suddenly whipping out, he gripped the rope, which the next minute was dangling from his hands and in front of Daniel's eyes. Swiftly now bringing his hands from behind him, Daniel tore the gag from his mouth, then spat out the threads before muttering, "I . . . I managed to get loose."

"Yes, yes, I see." The mate was nodding at him. "Cut

loose, oh yes, yes. I see. How did you manage to get to your knife?"

"I . . . I didn't, not with a knife." His mind was racing now for a plausible explanation. Then, his eyes looking past the mate to where lay some twisted iron bars, he nodded toward them, saying, "I hitched over to them and . . . and rubbed my hands against them."

The mate said nothing to this, but, taking a step forward, he picked up the rope from behind Daniel and, after scrutinizing it, said, "Very clean cut for rubbing. You . . . you wouldn't have had a visitor, would you?"

"Visitor? No, no. I . . . I know nobody who'd visit me, at least kindly, on this ship."

"No, you're right there. At least I think you are." The tone was smooth, quiet, but it troubled Daniel much more than if the man had gone into a rage. And when he now said, "What am I going to do with you? Tie you up again?" Daniel put in quickly, "Please, I . . . I can't do anything down here, I . . . I can't escape. And . . . and I was in agony tied up like that and nearly choking. Please don't tie me up again."

"But what if you decided to defend yourself, say with one of those pieces of iron, eh?"

"There's only one person I'd want to do that to, and I couldn't promise that I wouldn't have a try at him at least."

The mate gave a small chuckle, then edged toward Daniel, saying, "You know something, boy? If you were to do that I'd stand by and watch you." His grin widened. "Anyway, it's time to turn in. Get what sleep you can, and if your friend Mr. Combo should pay you a private visit, I give you leave to defend yourself, eh?"

"Thank you."

"Funny"—the mate laughed now—"saying thank you to me. You are an odd boy. But then all English are odd. I had imagined the young of the waterfront were mostly like Jackie."

The mate now put his head back, drew in his lips, then nodded to himself before turning abruptly away and saying, "We'll be meeting again, boy. Sleep while you can."

Alone again in the darkness, Daniel felt sick. That last gesture of the mate's after Jackie's name was mentioned . . . had he given it away? Oh no. He prayed not, for Jackie was his only hope. Sitting back against the stanchion once more, he bit tightly down on his lip and began to pray to the God he remembered from his Sunday School days.

Fear being rampant in Daniel, it was easier for him to keep awake now. The more he thought about how the mate had reacted during those last minutes he was down here, the more Daniel felt sure the mate knew who had cut him loose. And so now there was the added worry of what would happen or had already happened to Jackie, and all through him. It was odd, when he came to think of it, how one small act could escalate into tragedy. If he had obeyed his mother and not laid so much stress on the irritation and boredom that a weekend with her and her new husband would produce, none of this would have happened. He had only himself to blame. And if Combo was determined to put an end to him, which seemed to be the case, he didn't want to go knowing that he was being the cause of the same thing likely happening to Jackie. In the short time they had been together he knew that he had come to like him very much; he was the kind of fellow he would like for a friend, and he had proved he was the kind that would stand by you in a tight corner. And that was the point that was worrying him. Would Jackie have to pay too dearly for his help? Oh, in a way he wished they would hurry up and get it over with, whatever they were going to do to him. And if Jackie didn't put in an appearance before the sound of the ship's engine vibrated through the stinking hold, he would know then, all right.

It seemed a week . . . a month, a year, before he next heard the hatch being lifted. He couldn't believe either his eyes or his ears when he saw Jackie standing before him. But there was no merry grin on the young man's face now as he said, "You ready? It's later than I expected; they didn't change watch when they should have. I'm . . . I'm a bit worried. It's the mate. He looked at me strangely last night afore turning in. He laughed and had his soft voice on. He's dangerous when he talks soft, so . . . so I'm comin' with you."

"You are?"

"Aye; he'll know it was me who let you go and although he mightn't throw me overboard, I'll bet there'll come a moment when I'll wish he would. He has his way, has the Swede. So come on . . . But wait. You'd better know we'll have to swim for it, for Ryan and Miller are on the port side facing the quay. You'll find the water icy first thing in the morning. Anyway, keep close to me. I can swim like a duck, and if you don't struggle I'll get you to the bank all right—that's if you find you can't make it yourself. . . . And there's another thing. Once we get up on deck, step out of your boots. Boots are heavy goin' in the water."

"I've got shoes on and they're light. . . ."

"Shoes, boots, clogs, the only thing that'll get you through in the water besides your feet are flippers. Anyway, don't argue."

"I'm not, I was only . . ."

"Come on, it's light, a bit too light, but there's been a lot of hustle-bustle on board. I'd like to think they were tidying up for the captain comin', for things get a bit slack when he's not around. Anyway, should they by any chance rush us, get over the rails and jump. And when you're in the water, make as much hullabaloo as you can—there's bound to be workmen around somewhere, or perhaps the river police on patrol. Let's hope. But otherwise do everything as quiet as possible, even breathin'. And for God's sake"—he was halfway up the ladder now and he turned his head around and looked down on Daniel, whispering, "don't sneeze, whatever you do. Folks who've been down here find their nose is affected by the fresh air. Well, nip it, anything, but don't let it go. Understand?"

"Yes, yes, I understand."

Daniel's heart was thumping against his ribs so hard that he imagined someone was more likely to hear that than his sneezing. But when his head emerged through the hatch and he found himself in a sort of passageway, the end of which opened out into an area filled with machinery, he drew in a sharp breath, then found he had to nip his nose tightly to quell the pricking that normally preceded a sneeze.

Jackie now was moving stealthily forward; his hand pushed back behind him was touching lightly on Daniel's coat. But when it moved swiftly and gripped his arm, Daniel by instinct stepped back into the shadow of a doorway close to Jackie, only just in time to watch a man descending another ladder at the end of the short passage. Had he turned to the right when he reached the foot of it, the man would have instantly become aware of them, but he turned the other way toward the machinery.

Some seconds elapsed before Jackie gave the signal to move, and then they moved quickly but silently toward the ladder.

Like a monkey, Jackie skimmed it; but try as he might, Daniel couldn't emulate him for his limbs were still stiff and cramped, even though at intervals during the night he had exercised them. And as Jackie hauled Daniel up the last rungs and onto an open ironwork platform there was an impatient look on his face.

As they moved silently along the platform Daniel could see the man below bending over a machine and he felt his heart jump almost into his throat when the man stood up and turned about. He had only to raise his eyes and they would be lost, but after a couple of steps he was bending over another piece of machinery.

At the end of the platform three steps led to a door, and when Jackie quietly pushed it open there was the bright morning sky and real fresh air, and there, seemingly almost within touching distance, were warehouses on the far side of the quay. There was no sign of life on the quay, but between themselves and the quay was half a width of the ship and cabins and strange structures.

Jackie's hand on his neck suddenly brought him down onto his haunches and, as he must have crawled when a child, Daniel was now following Jackie in a crab walk alongside a cabin, then past a high structure with steps leading up to it from the side.

When they had rounded the steps, Jackie signaled Daniel to stop; then in sign language he pointed to a section of rail toward the bow of the boat and, putting his mouth to Daniel's ear, he whispered, "Near the lifeboat, I fixed a rope. It'll help you down. Do it as quietly as you can. When I give you the signal, make a run for it but keep low. . . . Take your shoes off now."

The seconds were being thumped out against his ribs but strangely he didn't feel afraid anymore. In a few minutes he would be free and once in the water he'd swim. Oh yes, he'd swim, if it meant the whole width of the river.

"Now!" Jackie silently mouthed the word, and then they were both running . . . two, three, four, five, six steps. They were almost there when the world exploded, but it did so without any noise as Daniel found his arms pinned in a steely grip and his body lifted from the ground. He was aware at the same time of the mate's dangling Jackie by the shoulders. It looked as if he was handling a suit of clothes without a body inside.

The next thing he was aware of as his captors swung him around was the hated face of Combo. The man was standing with his back to the rails and he was laughing.

It was too much.

As the men once again heaved him upward, taking his feet from the ground, he experienced a surge of anger that flowed through him like a great strength. Tensing his body, he drew back his legs, then thrust them forward. When his feet caught Combo in the stomach he had a wonderful satisfaction that mounted to elation as he saw the man's body double up like a concertina, sway for a moment, and then fall backward through the opening to the side of the davits holding the lifeboat. As Combo went he took with him a high screeching cry that was cut off abruptly by a splash.

"Good God!"

"He's over!"

"Quiet! Quiet!" That was the mate's voice. "A lifebelt!"

Daniel was surprised to find himself standing free while Jackie, he saw, remained in the steely grip of the mate. He noticed that Jackie was no longer struggling but seemed submissive; that was until he saw Jackie's eyes flicking to the corner while his head moved slowly to the side.

The mate's face was turned away. He was calling directions to three other crew men who had joined them, and when one of them, hanging over the rail, said, "He can't hold on much longer," the mate shouted, "Go down and get him, you Carlos. You swim good. It'll be quicker than lowering the boat."

In the meantime Daniel had picked up the message from Jackie and slowly and carefully backed away along by the wheelhouse. At this point he turned about and scampered along the deck, but when he reached the rail on the starboard side he saw that he could never jump to the quay—the distance was too wide. But there, farther along, was the gangway. It was down and there was no one near it—at least not at the head of it—but on the quay a car had drawn up. Daniel took no notice of the car; there wasn't time to think. He only knew he had to make the gangway and leap down it.

He reached it—his feet were actually on it—then he came to an abrupt stop. His hands extended to each side of him, gripping the iron handrails, he stood transfixed, his mouth agape as he stared downward.

There at the foot of the gangway was a man. But for his height he could have been twin to the mate, for both in body and face he resembled him. Ascending the gangway, the man came to stop a few feet from Daniel and he looked at him for a moment. Then looking to the side, he said to someone who had apparently appeared on the deck, "What's this?" His voice was thick and guttural.

"Mate'll explain, Captain," the voice behind called.

The captain moved toward Daniel now and, placing his hand flat on his chest, he pressed him backward up onto the deck. Once again Daniel was seized, only to be released almost instantly as the captain, turning and looking quickly along the length of the quay, growled, "Let him go. Do you want visitors?" Then addressing Daniel, he said, "Go along, boy." And Daniel went along, pushed by a hand that seemed as hard as iron.

A minute later he was in a cabin, together with Jackie.

"It was the carcasses, Captain," the mate was saying. "The little fellow brought 'em, and that lad along with 'em. He had found out about the racket, and more, because the little fellow means to make an end to him."

"Oh, he does, does he? And how does he mean to go about it? Tell me."

"Dumping him when we get out."

"Oh." The captain bobbed his head now, and his face became very red as he spat out words in his own tongue to the mate, who then, without making any comment whatever, went out. And now the captain was looking at Jackie, saying, "Why you do this? I thought I could trust you."

"Well"—Jackie bristled now as he spoke fearlessly—"I wasn't goin' to see that little squirt kill the lad. If you had been aboard, you would have seen to the matter, but you weren't here, were you?"

"So you took matters into your own hands and played captain, eh? Played the brave rescuer. And it would make you feel better, too, because he's twice your size."

"Aye, he might be, Captain, but he's still only a kid, not sixteen yet."

The captain now turned his gaze on Daniel as he said, "Fifteen years old—mighty good length for fifteen. You only fifteen, boy?"

"I'm nearly sixteen, sir."

"But you're still fifteen?" After a moment's hesitation Daniel muttered, "Yes, sir." And then they all turned toward the door to see the mate assisting Combo into the cabin. He was wrapped in a blanket and it was evident that he was shivering, which came over in his voice when, catching sight of Daniel, he stammered, "You . . . you . . . you young sw . . . swine, you!" and made toward him.

"Hold on!" The captain's hand went out and pulled Combo to a stop. Turning and looking up at the captain, Combo blurted out, "Tried . . . he . . . he tri . . . tried to do me in."

"Well, from what I hear, tit for tat, as you say. That's what you intend for him, is it not?"

Seeming for the moment to forget to whom he was speaking, Combo growled, "That's my business." And on this the captain swung him around by the shoulder, yelling now, "Your business! You forget yourself, little man. This is my ship."

"Aye, and you forget yourself too, Captain." Combo shrugged himself away from the captain's hold and, pulling one hand from the blanket, he pointed to Daniel as he said, "He could have us sent to prison."

"You mean he could have you sent to prison." The captain was glaring at Combo now but Combo, seeming to have become utterly fearless, cried, "You don't get prizes in this country for buying stolen sheep."

The captain now turned to the mate and again spoke rapidly in his own tongue. The mate answered him likewise while looking toward Combo, then with a half grin on his face he said in English, "Little men with big mouths eat themselves. Come on."

"What's this! I ain't goin' anywhere. What I mean is . . ."

"I know what you mean is." The captain nodded at Combo; then turning to the mate again, he said, "Tie them all up until we get out. We'll move straightaway if the tide's all right."

As the three of them were hustled out of the cabin, Combo yelling obscenities at the mate while two sailors escorted Daniel and Jackie, a man came running along the deck and whispered something in the mate's ear.

"Let the captain know," the mate said, at the same time turning Combo in the opposite direction and pushing him along the deck. When Combo retaliated by yelling loudly, the mate clapped a hand over his mouth and almost lifted him from his feet. Daniel, being pushed as swiftly behind him, knew a moment of hope. Could it be possible that somebody had actually found out where he was? Else why the change of direction from the starboard side? He turned his head and glanced at Jackie and something in the young fellow's face seemed to confirm his opinion. And so, five minutes later when, gagged and bound again, he lay in the bilges, accompanied now by Jackie and Combo, the look in whose eyes seemed to say he must have gone mad, he did not feel so hopeless.

But hope died finally sometime later. Could it have

been half an hour, or more? He couldn't guess, but when a shudder went through the ship and when the throbbing of the engines beat on his ears, he felt they were past saving. They were on their way out, finally.

11

It was five o'clock in the morning and Mr. Jones was standing at the open farmhouse door looking into the yard. It should have been light but everywhere was enveloped in a thick mist, as thick as any fog he had seen. If his lad had been lying out in that all night on the fells there was little hope that he would survive, for even now the air was like ice on the breath.

Mrs. Everton's voice, saying, "Come and have this cup of tea, Peter," caused him to turn from the door, which he now closed. Going into the kitchen, he looked to where Michael was getting into a duffle coat.

"I'm going to see to the beasts," Michael said by way of explanation. "It's a bit early but once it's clear we'll start looking again. John Craig and Arthur should be along shortly."

Peter Jones said nothing but sat down at the table and sipped at the cup of hot strong tea.

However, before he had finished the cup of tea he suddenly stood up again and exclaimed, "I'll go and help Michael. I must do something, I'll go mad just sitting here." And Mrs. Everton was about to reply when Sally's voice broke in on them from the stairway, crying, "Mom! Mom!"

Mrs. Everton ran into the small hall, there to meet her daughter halfway on the stairs, and to Sally's gabbled question of, "What time is it?" she said, "It's five o'clock in the morning, dear. Go back to bed."

"No! No!" Sally pushed past her and ran down the remaining stairs. At the foot she turned to her mother and said, "Is . . . is Daniel back? Did you find him?"

"No, dear, not yet."

"I've . . . I've remembered. I've remembered." She now ran to Mr. Jones, who had followed Mrs. Everton into the hall, and, slapping his sleeve, she said, "The old house. I . . . I found him in the old house. I . . . I mean, I had . . . had a turn." She now looked at her mother and put her hand to her brow and closed her eyes for a moment; and Mrs. Everton, leading her into the kitchen, said, "Come to the fire, dear. Sit down and tell us. Now . . . now think quietly and tell us."

Sitting before the fire, Sally looked from Mr. Jones, who was on his haunches before her, to her mother, who was kneeling by her side, and said, "Some . . . somebody grabbed me and I must have had a turn. And . . . and then, it . . . it was like a dream, and . . . and when I woke up there was Daniel. He was all tied up and gagged. He had woken me up and I couldn't think clearly. You know what I'm like, Mom."

"Yes, dear. Yes, dear. Go on."

"Well, he made me go . . . go out and come and tell you. But I was very . . ." She shook her head. "I don't know, I must have fallen asleep."

"Where was this, dear?"

"The old house. You know, Mom."

Her mother didn't answer, for she was already running to the back door shouting, "Michael! Michael!" And when Michael appeared through the mist she gabbled, "Get the car out. Sally's remembered. Daniel's in the old house."

"What?"

He was pushing past her into the kitchen now, which made her turn on him almost angrily, saying, "Don't waste time."

And his reply was almost as angry as he said, "Look, Mom, that was yesterday. If she knows he was in the old house, there is more to it."

Striding up to Sally, who was standing near Mr. Jones now, and his voice somewhat more controlled, he said, "What's this about Daniel being in the old house, Sally? Now try and think clearly: when did you see him?"

Sally blinked, bit on her lip, then said, "I . . . I remember going out looking for him. Then . . . then I was looking through the window of the old house, thinking that he might have sheltered there, when . . . when somebody grabbed me. Yes"—she nodded now from one to the other—"I remember that, somebody grabbing me. And then like—" her head drooped before she went on, "like as usual, things went blank and when I woke up I thought it was Mom shaking me." She looked at her mother. "I couldn't pull myself together. And then . . . and then I saw—" She blinked rapidly again and now nodded vigorously as she said, "That's when I saw him. He was all tied up and . . . and gagged." She now closed her eyes tightly, screwing them deep into the sockets as she endeavored to remember, and they all waited in silence until presently she said, "He kept pushing me, with his feet, and . . . and the next thing I remember was pulling a rag out of his mouth and him talking at me. But . . . but I was very tired. He said something about a—" She shook her head and then looked at her mother and said, "Oh, Mom!"

"It's all right, dear. It's all right. Just be quiet and try to think back."

Again there was a silence for some seconds before Sally burst out with the word, "Ship!"

"Ship?" They all repeated the word and she nodded and said, "Yes, that was it. He said Billy . . . Combo was going to put him on a ship."

"Combo!" They all spoke together. Then Mr. Jones said, "Did he say where?"

He was on his haunches again in front of Sally, holding her hands tightly but saying softly, "Which part of the river? Can you remember? Newcastle, North Shields, South Shields, which part?"

Sally shook her head. "I . . . No, I can't just . . . He said a ship and he kept telling me to go home. And I didn't want to because I was so tired."

Mr. Jones now rose to his feet and, looking at Michael, said, "Let's go. If he's not in that old house, and I doubt that by now, it's a matter for the police."

"Can I come with you?"

"No, no, don't be silly." Mrs. Everton had hold of Sally's arm.

"I'm not being silly, Mom . . . *Shields.*"

"What?" Both Mr. Jones and Michael turned about from the hall doorway and looked back into the kitchen, and again Michael said, "What?"

"Shields. That's where the ship is . . . ship and Shields. You remember, Mom"—she turned to her mother—"Dad used to say if you want to remember something pick a letter in the alphabet it starts with or . . . or tack it onto something quite opposite."

Both Michael and Mr. Jones were in front of Sally again and Mr. Jones, bending toward her, said, "You're sure it was Shields?"

"Well, the word popped into my mind, and . . . and I don't know about Shields. I've never been there."

"It could be." Mr. Jones was looking at Michael now. "All kinds of ships dock there. Don't let's waste any more time. Come on. . . ."

A few minutes later they were in the Land-Rover and bowling toward the old cottage. In the outhouses they found all the evidence they wanted of the sheep stealing, for there were at least twenty skins lying around. The door to the house itself was locked but Michael broke the back window and they went through the rooms. However, as they had expected they found nothing.

Once they reached the military road Michael drove at breakneck speed, taking the great dips in the road in a way that caused Mr. Jones to hold his breath, while at the same time gripping his seatbelt. At Chollerford they took the Hexham road and soon were on the highway to Newcastle. Their progress through the city was held up by the early morning traffic. Although it was only seven o'clock the city was thick with cars and trucks. However, on the coast road they were able to speed again toward the Tyne tunnel. Through this and they were into Jarrow. Then came Tyne Dock.

Here they stopped near the dock gates and Michael said, "We should inquire how to get onto the waterfront; this place has changed since I was here two or three years ago. They've taken the old arches down and it looks as if they've knocked half the dock buildings down as well."

"There's a man standing near the barrier." Mr. Jones pointed. "Best bet is to ask him. What do you think?"

"Yes, of course."

They alighted from the car and made their way to where the man was standing. It was Mr. Jones who spoke first. "Excuse me," he said, "but could you tell us how to get down to the waterfront?"

"You mean the pier, Shields pier?"

"Is that where the boats are berthed?"

The man grinned now, saying, "No, you'll find no boats berthed along there. It's this end you want for berths." He jerked his head backward.

"What ship are you looking for?"

Mr. Jones and Michael exchanged glances, and then it was Michael who now said, "We really don't know. You see, Mr. Jones's son"—he inclined his head sideways—"has been kidnapped by some sheep stealers." He paused now as the grin slid from the man's face, to be replaced by an expression that implied, "Oh yes? Tell me another."

"It's true." Mr. Jones's voice was stiff now. "We are from a hill farm back in Northumberland. We know that a number of sheep were stolen and skinned and brought down to a ship lying somewhere along this dock. My . . . my son happened to come across the thieves and he was taken along with them."

Again the expression on the man's face altered, but his words still held doubt when he said, "How do you know they're going to be shipped?"

"My . . . my sister overheard them," Michael put in now. "It . . . it was last night She managed to escape, but got . . . got lost in the mist and we didn't find her for hours."

The man did not voice his disbelief but nodded, then said, "I'm only the gatekeeper. Your best best is to contact the river police."

"How do we do that?" asked Mr. Jones.

"Well, you go along there." The man pointed to where a blacktop road began. "Some way along, about half a mile, you'll come to a cabin. That's the new River Police Headquarters for this end. They'll likely be able to sort things out for you."

"Thanks. Thanks." Mr. Jones and Michael answered in unison, then at a run they made for the road, which was bordered by neat stacks of timber.

They were both out of breath when they saw the police cabin and were just in time to see two river policemen emerging.

It was with some natural scepticism that the two policemen at first listened to the garbled story, started by Mr. Jones and frequently interrupted by Michael. But when it was finished the policemen looked at each other and the elder one said, "It could be. Might be something in it. Could be linked with that truck going out of the top gate. I thought it was funny, a truck along there on a Saturday night, but I couldn't do much about it as the fog was so thick. Well, let's go and have a look. We'll try the riverside jetty first."

"There's only three lying there," said the young policeman. "Would you think any of those could be up to tricks of this sort?"

"Not the Russian," said the other. "I shouldn't think anyway. There's the tanker, but she's only waiting to go into dock for repairs. That leaves the Swedish tramp. He's quite a regular, but always with a moldy-looking crew. And when we are talking of her"—he now looked toward the river—"she's due out on the tide and it's coming up to full now . . . come on!"

They were hurrying over the lock gates now, and there before them stretched the riverside jetty. Slowly moving away from it was a boat.

"That's her!" said the elder policeman.

"How you going to stop her? On what grounds?" said his companion.

"On what we've been told, I hope."

When they reached the quay opposite the boat, its bow was slowly turning toward the middle of the river, and on its bridge the captain was clearly to be seen.

When the first policeman hailed him, he put his head out of the window and called, "What did you say?"

"I said, will you please stop. I wish to board you."

"You wish to board me? Why?"

As the policeman paused for a moment Michael, who had been looking about him, suddenly stooped and picked up something from the ground; then excitedly he exclaimed, "Look! Wool. Sheep's wool. And hessian. They would put them into sacks. They couldn't have been skinned properly. . . . And look there!" He pointed to the grimy ground. "There's more. It isn't likely they usually buy their stores, I mean their meat, with the wool still on, not for on board."

The policeman made no comment on this, but calling

up to the captain now, he demanded, "I order you to turn about."

"What you say? I can't hear you."

The boat continued to move and when the captain's face disappeared from view, the policeman sprinted toward the lock bridge. But before following his mate the second one turned and called to Michael and Mr. Jones, "Stay where you are!"

Mr. Jones and Michael stood where they were and watched the boat straighten out. Then, as it went to head downriver, Michael cried, "Look! The police launch." And there she was, moving fast from the quayside. A minute later she crossed the bow of the boat and became lost to their sight.

They seemed to hold their breath for an interminable time, and then they glanced brightly at each other as they saw the boat begin to turn in the middle of the river. When its bow was pointed once again toward the quay, they both spoke together, saying, "They've done it!" Then Mr. Jones added, "Pray God we're on the right track."

"I second that," muttered Michael now, "because if we're not, we're in for trouble."

They could hear the captain's voice ranting long before the boat came alongside again, but before she touched the dock the river police were out of their launch and standing beside Mr. Jones and Michael.

When the captain stopped talking in his own tongue to someone behind him in the wheelhouse, the first policeman called up to him, "I'd like to come aboard, Captain."

"Why you wish to come aboard?" the captain now yelled.

"Just a little inquiry, sir, concerning these two gentlemen here." The policeman indicated Mr. Jones and Michael.

"Yes? Well, what would you like to know?"

Before the policeman had time to answer, Mr. Jones called up, "I'd like to know if you have my son aboard!"

In a low mutter only audible to his companions, the policeman said, "That was a mistake. Please leave this to me."

"Has he signed on?" the captain called to Mr. Jones.

The policeman stared up at the captain for a moment before he said, "No, sir. As far as I can understand he is, I think, stowing away."

"A stowaway? Huh!" The captain gave a short laugh. "No stowaways on board my ship. I see to that always. Every nook and cranny is searched. Oh no, sir, no stowaways on board my ship. Put your mind at rest, sir." He was again looking directly down on Mr. Jones. "I have no stowaways."

"He may not have any stowaways but he's got Daniel. I'd lay my bottom dollar on that." The muttered words came from Michael and the policeman answered as low, "Well, you might lose. But, on the other hand, you might not. Some of these are shifty beggars."

They now watched the gangway being lowered and a number of the crew came to the ship's rails and stood looking down on them. Then a minute later the captain appeared at the top of the gangway, and when the two river policemen walked up toward him it was the elder one again who said, "We have your permission to come aboard then, Captain?"

"Yes, you have my permission, but I do not know what you are looking for. I tell you we have no stowaway. But then—" His manner now seemed to undergo a complete change as he said smoothly, "I would not know about that today because I must admit I only came aboard shortly before we let go. I . . . I was held up."

"Mr. Mate!" The captain now called to the Swede, who was standing some distance behind him. "You take these gentlemen and show them over my ship . . . everywhere."

The word "everywhere" caused not only Mr. Jones's spirits to drop but made him look toward Michael, and the glance they exchanged said, What have we done? Because they both knew that stopping and searching a foreign ship could, if they were proved to be in the wrong, cause quite a bit of bother, even perhaps international bother.

Mr. Jones and Michael now followed the policemen and the mate, who, in the captain's cabin, made great play of showing them the opened wardrobe and the inside of a chest. He did the same in his own quarters. And when he came to those of the crew, which were a series of cabins with three bunks in each, he also made great play of pulling down the bedrolls. Next he led them into the galley, where a cook was busy preparing food. After which they went through the storerooms.

As to the cargo, which was, he said, just crates of machinery, he ordered members of the crew to push back the hatches and invited the policemen to go down with him. At the same time he ordered Mr. Jones and Michael to stay where they were because landlubbers, he said, were apt to break their necks. They stayed where they were but their eyes scanned the deck, and when Michael went toward a ladder leading downward, one of the crew yelled, "Bide your time there, laddie. You could get lost if you go down there."

Michael turned a disdainful glance on the man before going back to where Mr. Jones was standing and muttered, "I . . . I've got a queer feeling on me."

"What kind of a feeling, other than we're on a wild goose chase?" Mr. Jones's voice was flat now.

"I . . . I don't think we're on a wild goose chase somehow. Look at them. Look at the way they're standing watching us. They're not acting like people with nothing to hide. Some of them look scared."

As Mr. Jones looked at those members of the crew who were scattered here and there on the deck, he thought, He's right. Then he turned his attention to the policemen who were coming up from the hold, and when they were on the deck he said immediately, "I think we should look below." But before either of the policemen could answer, the captain put in, "Nothing below but machinery."

"Well, we would like to see the machinery, if you don't mind." It was one of the first policemen speaking, and the mate, after staring at the captain, looked from one to the other before turning abruptly and leading the way toward the iron staircase.

A few minutes later they were all standing on the iron platform, looking down at the engines. They were still now and a man had his back to one as he stood staring up at them.

"You see"—the captain spread his arm wide—"there is nothing to see but machinery, nothing."

"Where does that lead to?" Michael was now pointing to where another iron staircase led down from the end of the platform, and the captain with a shrug of his shoulders said offhandedly, "Oh, that leads to a sort of storeroom and the bilges."

Almost before he had finished speaking the policemen were moving toward the ladder. Once down it, they made their way along a narrow passage that opened out into a small square like a landing. There was a door with an iron bar across it and the captain, going straight toward it, thumped on it angrily, saying, "Refrigerator."

"Yes, all right, it's a refrigerator. Would you mind opening the door, please?"

The captain's jaw worked from side to side; then, motioning to the mate, he said abruptly, "Open." And when the door of the refrigerator was pulled wide, the captain switched on a light and pointed inward to a small square room that looked almost bare except for half a side of beef, a pig hanging on hooks from the roof, and some small cuts of beef and rolls of sausages on a shelf to the side.

"You satisfied?" The captain glared at them now and with another wave of his hand ordered that the mate should close the door.

"How do you get down to the bilges?" It was the second policeman asking the question, and neither the captain nor the mate answered for a moment. Then it was the mate who said, "Bilges? There's nothing down there but rats and stink. You should know what bilges are."

"Yes, we know what bilges are"—the policeman nodded toward them—"and we would like to see yours."

He turned from the mate and looked at the captain, whose color had changed now to almost purple. But it was the first policeman who spoke quietly, saying, "I think you had better let us see the bilges, Captain. If there's nothing there, then we'll be satisfied and you can turn about once more, but if there is anything there that shouldn't be—you know what I mean—and you obstruct our search, then . . . well"—he paused—"I have no need to enlarge, have I?"

They all watched the captain swallow deeply; they watched him turn his head from side to side; then he almost began to gabble, "I have just come on board. As I said, I have been on leave. No more than an hour I have been here. What has happened has happened in my absence, you will note. You will note, do you hear, that what has happened has happened in my absence? My mate will explain . . ."

The mate had taken a step backward now and was glaring at the captain, saying, "Be damned if I take blame. I do not buy sheep. I know nothin' of little fellow and what his game is." He now turned and looked from Mr. Jones to Michael, adding, "The boy, I know nothing about him; it was the little man. I keep them here and await orders." He now turned an angry glance on the captain, who, biting hard on his lower lip, closed his eyes for a moment before saying grimly, "Open the hatch."

Slowly the mate backed from them, then, turning about, moved along another passageway, at the end of which he bent down and slowly lifted up an iron hatch. When he went to back away from it, the first policeman said, "Go on down." And he motioned him forward again. Then turning to his own companion, he added, "Stay with him." And now he was nodding toward the captain.

One after the other they followed the mate down into the bilges, and all were affected by the stench and the sight that met their eyes.

* * *

Daniel had given up all hope when he had heard the engines start up and felt the motion of the ship underway. Then when the ship seemed to stop he felt Jackie bump him twice in the shoulder. He wasn't sure what message Jackie was trying to convey. But when the engines started up again, the flicker of hope died away, until a short time later—he had no idea how long—the engines again stopped, dead this time. And now Jackie continued to bump him.

The waiting in the blackness seemed endless before he saw the hatch being lifted and the light shining down on them, followed by a row of figures he couldn't as yet recognize.

He was so tired and weary, cramped and fear-filled, that for a moment he imagined he had gone funny in the head, because in the wavering light he now thought he was seeing the mate, together with a policeman and his father and Michael.

Then the place became flooded with light, and there were voices and hands all over him. Then his father was holding him close and he was crying. Everybody was talking, seemingly all of them at once. He heard Jackie saying, "He meant to murder the lad here. The sheep he brought on are over there, mucked up now. That's where they threw them when they got frightened."

"Come on, come on, lad," Michael was saying to Daniel, but he couldn't move. When they had strung him up last time they had bent this legs almost to his hands, and now he felt as if he wouldn't be able to walk again. He hoped he wasn't going to pass out; he had done that once before and once was enough.

"You're all right. You're all right." His dad was holding his face between his hands and Daniel managed to smile at him and for the first time spoke, saying, "Glad to see you, Dad." His father made no reply to this for he couldn't speak because of the tears of relief now choking him.

They were getting Daniel up the ladder now, pulling him up rung by rung. It felt more painful than being tied up.

It wasn't until he was on the top deck and saw one policeman leading Combo down the gangway and another policeman standing apart talking to Jackie that he seemed to come alive again and he shouted, "No, no!" Pulling himself from his father's arms, he stumbled toward Jackie, calling to the policeman as he went: "He tried to save me. That's why they were going to do him in too. You can't take him."

"Who's taking him?" The policeman smiled at him now. And like a deflated balloon Daniel said, "Oh, I'm sorry. I thought—" He looked at Jackie and Jackie grinned at him. And the policeman said, "We'll need you for a witness of course; you'll have to give me your address where I'm likely to find you."

Jackie looked at Daniel now, then to Michael, who was standing by his side, then to Mr. Jones before he again turned his gaze onto the policeman and said, "Well, it's like this. I've no address here except the Seamen's Mission. Aye. Aye, that's where you'll find me, the Seamen's Mission."

"No, you're coming home with me . . . with us. Can't he, Dad?" Daniel appealed to his father, and without hesitation Mr. Jones said, "Yes, yes of course. The address is 22 Baker Avenue, Newcastle." But he had hardly finished speaking before Michael put in, "You'd better take down another address because these two won't be there all the time during the next few weeks. It's Hillburn Farm, Brooks End."

The policeman smiled at him. "We'll find it. And you, young fellow"—he nodded now toward Jackie—"it's a good thing you changed camps or you'd be finding yourself along with this lot." And he moved his head, taking in the ship. "They'll only be able to get the captain on receiving stolen sheep. But I think the mate'll be in for more, as he was in charge when that little snipe came aboard. I should imagine that fellow'll be in for a long stretch."

"And not soon enough." Michael nodded at the policeman, his face and voice grim now. "The sheep stealing's been going on for the last two or three years, but there's more than him in it."

"Don't worry, they'll be caught. Well now"—the policeman closed his notebook—"I've got all the particulars I need at the moment but you'll be having visits from us before the case comes up, so you'd better get going and leave us to attend to the captain and his gentlemen crew. . . . Can you manage finding your sea legs, or your land legs, once again?"

The policeman was smiling at Daniel, and Daniel, looking at him, said quietly, "Yes, I can manage. And thank you. Thank you very much."

"And I endorse that." Mr. Jones nodded toward the policeman. "Oh, a thousand times."

"Oh, that's all right, it's all in a day's work. That's what we're here for. If these things didn't happen we'd be out of a job." He laughed now and led them toward the gangway.

Jackie was the last to leave the ship, and at the bottom of the gangway he looked back. And Daniel, seeing him standing still, said, "Are you sorry you're leaving her, Jackie?" And Jackie, after a moment, turned and answered truthfully, "Yes and no." Then with an impish grin he added, "But I'm glad I'm alive to be able to leave her."

Quietly now they all made their way back to the dock gates and to the waiting Land-Rover and drove away.

And there was no laughter or chatter between them for both Michael and Mr. Jones were aware it had only been by a thin thread of luck they had been able to find Daniel. And both Daniel and Jackie were aware it was little short of a miracle that they were sitting here alive and not lying in that stinking hold awaiting a death weighed down by iron bars that would have brought them to rest forever on the bottom of the ocean.

12

They all agreed that it was the strangest Sunday any of them had experienced. When they reached the farm Mrs. Everton had thrown her arms about Daniel and held him tightly to her as any mother might have. And as a son might have returned a mother's embrace, he clung to her until shyly he pulled himself away only now to be hugged by Sally. And this was beginning to be embarrassing when she too spilled her tears over him. But he was not brusque with her for he remembered that but for her, by what Michael had told him, he would surely have been dead this day.

Then followed the business of explaining Jackie's presence among them. Up till now Jackie had stood on the outskirts of what appeared to him to be a family ring. But Mrs. Everton's hands going out to him brought him into the circle.

It wasn't until late the same day when they were all sitting around the table enjoying a good meal that Mrs. Everton, looking across at Jackie, said, "Have you no one at all belonging to you, Jackie?" After a moment he replied, "No one that I'd bother about, Mrs. Everton, or who's likely to bother about me."

"Were you thinking about going back to sea?" she asked.

"Oh, no"—he moved his head—"not unless I can't get a job ashore. But then I'm not fitted for anything special. I had ideas about being a carpenter once but you had to have training for that."

"It's not too late." It was Michael speaking now, and Jackie, turning to him, grinned as he said, "I mightn't look it but I'm past eighteen, on the ship's papers."

"Well, there's always training places, technical schools and the like. Anyway, what Mom's leading up to, but she's so slow at it, is that we've talked it over and if it's all right with you, you can stay here until you get set with something. Of course, I'll take it out of your skin in making you do odd jobs around the place."

"You mean that?" Jackie's voice was soft as he looked from one to the other.

"Well, we wouldn't be saying it if we didn't. Anyway, that's settled." And abruptly now Michael turned his attention to Daniel. "Now how about you?" he said, and Daniel almost choked on a mouthful of food as he answered, "Me? What about me?"

"What are you going to do when you leave school?"

"Not be a farmer, that's certain." At this there was general laughter. Then as it died away Daniel said seriously, "You know, in the time I was tied up . . . was it a year, or twenty years?" He looked from one to the other. "It seemed like it by all the thinking I did. And you know, I wondered why I'd ever wanted to leave school. School appeared, on looking back, like paradise."

"What!" It was now Mr. Jones's turn almost to choke. "You mean you would consider staying on and making something of yourself?"

"What do you mean, making something of myself?" Daniel bridled in mock annoyance. "I am something, I am something already."

At this there was more laughter. And now Mrs. Everton said, "Of course you are, Daniel; you just want to be something better. Anyway, tell us what it is."

All eyes were turned on Daniel now. He looked down toward his plate as he said slowly, "I don't know, not really. I don't think I'm clever enough to be a doctor, nor yet a vet, because it's about the same training, but . . . but"—his head drooped lower—"I feel I want to do something to . . . well . . ."

"To help people?" Everyone's attention now slowly turned toward Sally. She was looking at Daniel and Daniel at her, and after a moment he admitted shyly, "Yes, yes, Sally, you're right. I suppose that's what I really want to do, something like that. Not that I'm feeling goody-goody. Don't get me wrong." He now looked defiantly around, then ended lamely, "Oh, I don't know. It sounds so silly. Anyway, who started all this?"

"You did." His father smiled at him.

And now Sally said, "My dad used to say, if you want a thing badly enough you'll get it. You just have to keep thinking about it all the time. I keep thinking about . . ." She gulped in her throat now and bit on her lip. And her mother, putting her hand out quickly, patted her arm and said gently, "Yes, yes, we know." Then she added briskly, "Well now, I think if we've all finished, there's washing up to be done, and drying up to be done. That's for those inside. And if I hear aright, there's cows mooing and chickens clucking and pigs saying, what about it?"

Amid laughter now they all rose from the table. As they did so there came the sound of a car being driven into the yard, and Mrs. Everton, going to the window, said, "That'll be the Newberrys. They phoned earlier." Then she half turned from the window, saying, "No, it isn't," and looked from Mr. Jones to Daniel before adding, "It's your mother."

Daniel stared back at her in silence. Forty-eight hours earlier his response would have been, "Oh Lord!" But as he had said, he had done a great deal of thinking since he had last seen his mother, thinking that was as yet muddled.

He looked at his father, and his father was looking at Mrs. Everton, and she, speaking solely to him, said, "Well, go and bring them in." And almost in the same breath she uttered her commands to her son: "You were talking about all the work you had to do outside. Well, it's still waiting. And for you too, Jackie."

When she pushed Jackie in the direction of the door, he laughed a deep rumbling laugh that seemed in no way connected with his thin wiry body; then he ran after Michael and joined him, and they both laughed.

Daniel remained in the kitchen. Presently his mother and stepfather entered, and mother and son stood looking over the distance at each other. And when she at last spoke, her voice had a cracked sound: "We . . . we heard about it on the radio," she said.

"Oh," he answered.

"Come and sit down. Have you had a meal?"

Clare Ancliff, as she was now, looked at Mrs. Everton and said, "Yes, thank you, we've eaten. But . . . but I wouldn't mind a cup of tea."

"Certainly. Certainly."

"You've had a rough time?"

Daniel turned and looked at his mother's husband. He'd always thought of him as "the man," but now he seemed to be seeing him in quite a different light. Perhaps he had changed, or, uncanny thought, was it himself who had changed?

Because he hadn't answered him, his father answered for him, saying, "Yes, that's the word, rough. He's lucky to be alive."

"A real hero, eh?"

That's what he didn't like about him, always coming out with things like that. But perhaps he was embarrassed. They were all embarrassed, his father most of all.

It was some minutes later, after both his mother and the man had drunk a cup of tea, when Mrs. Everton said to Mr. Ancliff, "You've never seen round our farm, have you?"

"No, no, I haven't."

"Would you like to have a look round?"

"Yes, I would very much."

Mrs. Everton went toward the kitchen door, and as Mr. Ancliff made to follow her he turned to his wife and said, "Would you like to come, Clare?" But she, looking up at him, answered, "If you don't mind, another time."

He nodded at her before turning away and following Mrs. Everton out into the yard.

"I was worried, worried sick." His mother was looking at his father, and he answered, "We all were, Clare."

"Perhaps . . . perhaps I . . . I was the cause, coming

like that, demanding." And she looked at Daniel, who could have answered truthfully, "Yes, you were," but what he said was, "I'll be back in a minute." Instead of making for the hall and the stairs, he walked into the sitting room, and once inside he stood with his back to the door, telling himself he couldn't bear it. That look on her face. He had never seen her look contrite like that in his life before. It . . . it wasn't her. And now her voice came to him, saying, "I've . . . I've done a lot of thinking since yesterday, Peter. Was it just yesterday that I was here?"

"Yes, it was just yesterday, Clare." His father's voice was soft.

"It was awful to think he would run away rather than be with me. I never thought I could be so hurt, not again. I never thought I would cry again, not like I did."

"I'm sorry . . . I'm sorry you felt like that."

"I've been a pig, haven't I? I was a pig to you."

"It's all past now. Don't let it worry you any more."

"It should, and it will. All I wanted in those early years were things, things to give me comfort, things that money could buy. Now . . . well, I have them all."

"Don't cry, Clare. Please don't cry. . . . I thought you'd be happy, that he was what you wanted."

There was a long silence now, and Daniel bit tight on his lip as he waited. And when her answer came he bowed his head down to his chest at the meaning behind her words. "He's all right," she said; "it isn't his fault. It's just that . . . well, things are just things. You can soak in a scented bubble bath all day but you're still left with your mind."

"Oh, Clare." His father's voice was weighed deep with compassion.

"It's all right. It's all right."

There was another long pause before his mother's voice came again, saying softly now, "I . . . I thought that if I had Daniel, that if I could give him all the things that I had wanted, he would at least . . . well, love me a little. I . . . I knew I didn't deserve it, I'd neglected him; but let alone loving me, he doesn't even like me. I've had to face up to that too. Two different things, you know, Peter, loving and liking. Yet they're both entwined: you can love somebody and hate them, but if you like them you can never hate them. And the funny thing is"—now her voice rose—"you know, Bill thinks the world of Daniel. He likes him. Yes, he likes him. He couldn't feel more for him if he was his own. And the pity of it is I know that Daniel can't stand him." There followed another painful silence before her voice came to Daniel again, saying, "It's always been my weakness, hasn't it, Peter, never to face up to things. But these last couple of days . . . oh dear, dear, have I seen myself as I really am! And as you must have seen me for years. I was a bitch to you. Oh, I was, but I'm paying for it."

As his father said pleadingly, "Please, please, Clare, no more; it's over and done," Daniel groped his way to a chair and, sitting sideways on it, he bent over the back and squeezed his eyes tightly in order to check the tears. Then his head jerked upward as a voice whispered, "You all right, Daniel?"

He looked about him for a moment, then toward the window at the end of the room. It was open and Sally was leaning over the sill. He remained seated, looking at her while rubbing his face roughly with his hand. And when she said, "What's the matter?" he rose and went toward the window. Looking down on her, he said hesitantly, "Nothing's the matter. I'm just tired."

Sally stared up at him for a moment before saying, "It's your mom and dad, isn't it? They're in the kitchen. They're talking about you. I heard a bit, but I wasn't intending to listen." She shook her head. "I was just meaning to go in to get some crusts for Sandy, but I came out again. They didn't see me. . . . Why don't you like your mother?"

"Who said I didn't like her?"

"Well, you don't act as if you do. And then running off yesterday. That's what caused all the trouble, you know." She nodded at him. "I . . . I can't understand anybody not liking their mom and dad."

"Then all I can say is, you've been lucky. And you have, you know."

"Yes, I have, but only in some ways." She turned her head now and looked back onto the strip of gravel that bordered the front of the house. Then, her voice very low, she said, "I haven't been all that lucky, have I? I'm not . . . I mean, I can't be like other girls."

As Daniel stood gazing down on her bent head he recalled the conversation at the table a little earlier, when he had shyly admitted he wanted to help people. . . . Well, here was someone who needed help. And in a blundering way he thought he was giving it when he said, "I can't see any difference. You are just the same as any other girl."

"Oh, don't be silly!" He was amazed at the anger in her voice and the look on her face. "I'm an epileptic, remember. People get afraid of you; they shy away; they're thinking all the time you're going to have a fit."

"That's nonsense!" His voice was as hard as hers now. "And anyway, Michael says yours have lessened with the years and that you're going for special treatment next month."

"Yes, yes." She sighed. "But I still yell when I have a turn. You've . . . you've heard me?"

"Yes, but Michael says—"

"Oh! Our Michael. Michael!" She shook her head impatiently. "Michael says one thing and Mom says another. Michael's for me facing up to it, Mom's for me hiding it. Oh, I know, I know." Again her head was shaking. "I think at times they must feel I'm stupid too . . . mental." She leaned further over the sill now and, her head back on her shoulders, she looked up at him as she said softly, "I want to face up to it. I want to go out and mix with people. Mom thinks I'll get hurt. Well, I know I shall. But there are people who understand, because I'm not the only one like this. There are thousands of us, and a lot are in good jobs. Michael says so. You know something?" She paused a moment, and when he made no reply she went on, "The first night you came here Michael wanted to tell you in case I had a turn, and I begged him not to. I slept up in the attic just in case. But then I did have a turn and you heard me, didn't you?"

All of a sudden Daniel found himself dropping to his haunches so that his face was on a level with hers, and what he said next surprised even himself; more so, it shook him, for some part of his mind protested: What's up with you, you gone crazy? For what he was saying was, "If I promise to go home for a few days with Mom, would you come along too, if your mother'll let you?"

There was no answer, for Sally, her mouth slightly open, her eyes wide, was gazing at him in stupefied silence, until he said loudly, "Well?"

"Do you mean that?"

He hardly heard her words, but he said, "I wouldn't say it if I didn't."

"But . . . but your mother, she mightn't . . ."

"You leave it to me. Go on about your business." He smiled broadly at her now and pushed her in the shoulder, and she backed away from the window. Then as he watched her put her hand tightly over her mouth, he was on the point of saying, "Oh, for heaven's sake, don't cry!" when she turned and ran from him along the side of the house and into the farmyard.

He himself now turned and moved slowly down the room to the door that led into the kitchen. But once there he paused and closed his eyes tightly for a moment. When his mother's voice came to him, saying, "Are you going to marry her?" his eyes sprang wide, and he waited for his father's answer. It came low and firm. "Yes," he said, "if she'll have me. But there's been no question of it yet; her husband's been dead but a short time."

His mother's voice came down to him like a soft whisper, saying, "I hope you'll be happy. You deserve it. And . . . and she's lucky."

Not being able to bear any more, he pulled the door open abruptly and marched into the kitchen. And there, looking at his father, he said, "I'm . . . I'm going back with Mom for a few days."

His father's eyes narrowed and he stared at him for some seconds before, his face moving into a slow smile, he said, "Good. I'm glad of that."

"That's if"—Daniel now turned to his mother—"that's if I may bring Sally along with me."

"Oh, yes, yes." Clare Ancliff's face took on a brightness as she repeated, "Oh yes, of course."

"She's epileptic. She has fits."

He watched the brightness seep from his mother's face as she repeated, "Fits?"

"Yes, fits. But should she have a turn, I could see to her."

There was a silence for a moment as they looked at one another. Then his mother spoke again, saying now, "I'll . . . I'll be pleased to have her. She seems a nice child."

"She's not a child, Mom, she's nearly fourteen. But as far as I can gather she's never had any outside life, I mean away from the farm. And she needs a break. You know what I mean?"

Once more the smile returned to his mother's face and it widened as she said, "Yes, I know what you mean."

At that moment Mrs. Everton and Mr. Ancliff came back into the room and it was to Mrs. Everton that Daniel now spoke. His words almost tripping over each other, he said, "I'm . . . I'm going back with my mother, Mrs. Everton, for a few days, and she says she'll be pleased to have Sally come along."

"Oh . . . Oh, I don't think that's . . ."

"That'll be fine. She'll enjoy that; do her the world of good. About time she got out and about." They all turned and looked to where Michael was standing with Jackie by his side. Michael was wiping his hands on a towel and he threw it to one side as he entered the kitchen. His eyes on his mother, he made straight for her and, putting his hand out, he touched her chin with his fingers, saying, "You think so, don't you? Best thing, give her a break?"

"But what if?"

"If there's any ifs, Mrs. Everton, I'll be with her."

Mrs. Everton looked across at Daniel now and said, "You can't be with her all the time, Daniel. What about at night?"

"If you'd care to leave that to me, she could have the room next to ours and . . . and I could see to her."

Daniel looked at his mother. They all looked at her. Her husband was now standing close by her side, and he put his arm around her shoulder as, looking at Mrs. Everton, he said, "She'll be fine, and we'd love to have her. So what are we waiting for? Let her get packed and come along, eh? What about it, Danny boy?"

Danny boy! Retaliation was rising in him but he checked it. This was one of the things he would have to get used to. He recalled his mother's words: "He thinks the world of him." Quickly he turned about, saying, "I'll go and find Sally."

Half an hour later they were all ready for departure. His mother and her husband were outside near the car, as were Sally and her mother and Michael. Jackie was standing a little apart. But in the kitchen Daniel was looking at his father, and Peter Jones, looking at his son, said softly, "Try to enjoy it. It'll help her, and him too."

"Danny boy!" Daniel screwed up his face, and his father laughed and said, "He means well. I'll give him that much. And you know something? Your grandmother always used to say, if a man talks nonsense, it's because he's either a fool or embarrassed or he's hurt. Well, that fellow's no fool and I don't know about being hurt, but I think his main trouble is embarrassment. I can understand that. Anyway, stay as long as you can."

"Not more than a week, Dad."

"Well, she'll be very satisfied with that, I'm sure. And Daniel"—his father now leaned forward and gripped his hand—"be nice to her, kind, forget about the past. Recrimination never helps the present or the future. Go on now. And don't forget about your charge: give her a good time. Take her to a dance."

"A dance, Dad?" Daniel screwed up his face. "But what if she was to have a . . .?"

"Well, what about it? They would think it was a new step. You know, to my mind that new kind of dancing appears as if they are all having fits."

"Oh, Dad." They pushed against each other, then went out in the yard. And the last one Daniel spoke to was Jackie.

"See you in a few days," he said. Jackie didn't answer for a moment, then quietly he replied, "Aye, see you in a few days. But afore you go I just want to say, ta, thanks for bringing me into the only real family I've ever known in me life. You know something? I don't think you'll ever have any trouble in finding a job: first me, and then her. Raiser of fallen hopes, you are. Just think of the things you could put in for: the police, the lifeguards, the samaritans. It's endless, man."

The push that Daniel gave him nearly knocked him on his back, and Daniel laughed as he said, "Yes, it could be the police, and the first thing I'd do would be to run you in, you fool."

"Come on. Come on." The orders came from the car, and when Daniel reached it he found that Sally was already sitting in the front next to Mr. Ancliff, and his mother was in the back.

No sooner had he taken his seat beside her than the car began to move, and Mrs. Everton walked beside it on one side, looking in apprehensively at her daughter, and Michael and Mr. Jones were on the other side, Michael with his usual quipping about people who could go off jaunting when all the work was to be done. But his father said nothing, he only looked in on him and the woman who had been his wife, and he nodded quietly to them both.

As the car went out of the gate and picked up speed Daniel looked at his mother. She was already gazing at him, and when her hand came out and caught his, the warmth that had been missing from his life for a long time seeped through him. And after a moment when she lay back against the seat and looked ahead, he did the same. And as he listened to Sally and Mr. Ancliff chatting away in the front, it came to him that he would never be afraid again, at least not of the things that had frightened him up till now, such as getting into a fight, and using his fists if it were necessary, for he felt suddenly whole, bigger, wider —not just lanky—and more understanding. Yes, more understanding. That was the important part. And what was more, as Jackie had said, he could be anything, do anything. It was up to him. Yes, it was up to him, Daniel Jones.

About the Author

CATHERINE COOKSON was born in Tyne Dock, England. She describes her childhood as "poor and hard, interspersed with flashes of wonder when thinking up tales to tell a captive audience." She left school at age thirteen and continued her education on her own, using the public library as her university.

Mrs. Cookson's first book was published in 1950, and she now has over fifty books in print, some for young readers. Her two previous Lothrop books were *Mrs. Flannagan's Trumpet* and *Go Tell It to Mrs. Golightly*. She lives in Norththumberland, England.